RECLAIMING
Izabel

VICTORIA PAIGE

Reclaiming Izabel
Copyright © 2025 by Victoria Paige
All rights reserved.
Print ISBN: 979-8-9889501-4-1

2nd Edition

No part of this book may be reproduced in any form or by any electronic or mechanical means, including information storage and retrieval systems, without written permission from the author, except for the use of brief quotations in a book review.

This book is a work of fiction. The characters, names, places, events, organization either are a product of the author's imagination or are used fictitiously. Any similarity to any persons, living or dead, business establishments, events, places or locale is entirely coincidental. The publisher is not responsible for any opinion regarding this work on any third-party website that is not
affiliated with the publisher or author.

Editor: Erica Russikoff, Erica Edits
Cover Designer: Deranged Doctor Design

author's note

This second edition of Reclaiming Izabel has been reworked to first-person POV. The storyline remains the same compared to the original but with enhancements to fit the new perspective.

chapter
one

Drake

The smell of antiseptic hit me first. I blinked my eyes open, but everything was so fuzzy, I could only make out the acoustic tiles on the ceiling. My gaze wandered, and an IV line came into view.

Monitors beeped.

A hospital.

The lower half of my body was numb.

I panicked. The dull roar of pain was familiar. I'd been pumped full of painkillers.

My breaths came quick and shallow.

The monitor beat spiked.

I was in a nightmare.

A woman in green scrubs rushed in. She peered into my face before leaning over me.

"Where am I?"

She didn't answer.

"Where the fuck am I?" I gritted more forcefully.

Then horror rushed in.

The firefight.

Our retreat into the caves.

The blast.

My team incinerated right before my eyes.

No.

Dead. All my men were dead.

A roar.

A bellow of anguish.

Pain in my chest.

A pinprick on my arm.

Oblivion.

When I next came to, a man with close-cropped blond hair was leaning against the wall beside my bed. Tall, muscular, with strong, angular features and ice-blue eyes I would recognize anywhere.

The eyes of a killer.

"Viktor?" I croaked. "What are you doing here? Where am I?"

"Where you are is not important," he replied.

"Fuck you..." I swallowed, throat parched. "Tell me...fuck..."

Each breath was excruciating.

"Your back's broken. Your right leg is fractured in three places. Your right hand is a mess. I could go on...hopefully, you're not half-blind. If so, you're useless to me."

What. The. Fuck.

"Start making sense—"

"If you'd stop interrupting—"

"My team…"

A flicker of sympathy flashed through Viktor's face. "Dead."

"My commander…"

The last thing I remembered was shielding Commander Harrelson when we realized all our attackers wore suicide vests.

"He's the lone survivor," Viktor acknowledged. "Both of you were lucky to be caught in an air pocket among the rubble. He's on his way back to the U.S." He paused. "Although he'd prefer it if he'd died."

My eyes narrowed.

"We just received word that his wife and sons were killed in a car accident."

Foreboding settled in my gut and, even under the influence of painkillers, my brain refused to believe in coincidences.

Viktor's next words confirmed my fears. "Your team was targeted."

My wife. "Izabel…does she know I'm here?"

"She'll be informed of your death."

No.

"Get out," I rasped.

"Listen, Lieutenant."

"Get the fuck out of here!" My chest was caving in as I tried to drag air into my lungs. It fucking hurt.

"The men responsible for your team's massacre will only

leave Izabel alone if you're dead," Viktor gritted through his teeth. "Harrelson's survival hasn't been made public yet, but intel is buzzing that Fire Team families are in danger. Can't explain. We're outta time. Delaying the release of the KIA list will put SEAL families in danger. Do you understand, Maddox?"

"Izabel—"

"My people are keeping her safe."

"I want to talk to her."

"Listen, Maddox." Viktor stepped closer to my bed. "Make a decision. Or let the DoD give you and Izabel new identities. You've got months of recovery ahead of you. You can't protect her. You can't shoot for shit. You're a liability. Do you think Uncle Sam's gonna foot the bill and hire you security? You know that's bullshit and, if you don't act now, it'll be too late."

My brain was squeezing out of my skull at the enormity of the decision facing me. I couldn't be dead to Izabel. It'd kill her. It *would* kill me.

"I want you on my task force," Viktor pressed on. "We'll give you time to heal. The doc said your spine will heal in two months. Full recovery in six. You'll be back in fighting form, but Drake Maddox needs to be dead for this to happen."

Rage burned through me, and I cursed my physical helplessness.

"I'm not abandoning my wife!" I gritted through my teeth.

"It's possible to return to her." Viktor paused. "We have no idea how long this mission can take. It could be a year; it could be five. Any inkling you're alive endangers her. Best if she moves on."

"You're out of your fucking mind."

Viktor blew out a breath and the way the man regarded me gave me chills.

"She's pregnant."

I didn't even question how Viktor knew. Joy burst in my heart, but, just as quickly, it shattered into unbearable pain even worse than my broken body.

"You return to her as is, both of you would be on the run, wondering if each day would be your last. Is that the life you want for her and your unborn child?"

"As opposed to making her a widow?" My voice was guttural with the sense of overwhelming loss, but a decision had solidified in my gut. My throat scraped like I'd swallowed a boxful of tacks. "I need people I can trust to watch over her."

"My agents—"

"My people, Viktor," I growled.

"One person," Viktor relented.

"No."

"Only one person outside our task force can know you're alive," he stated unequivocally. "I'd have to vet him. If he doesn't pass, there's no compromise. If you refuse to become a ghost, I'm turning you over to Joint Special Operations Command."

His warning wasn't lost on me. The moment I stepped out of the secretive world of Viktor Baran, I'd be exposed, and Izabel could be dead before I reached her.

"Hank," I muttered, and then more loudly, "Hank Bristow."

———

Izabel

I had been crying for two days after reports of a special ops team massacre hit the SEAL community. And if that news wasn't terrible enough, Jessica—the wife of Drake's CO—had been killed in a car accident together with her young boys. Rumors were rampant that SEAL families were in danger, but they had been squelched by the Navy's communications director. I'd come home this morning after sitting vigil all night at one of the wives' homes where we'd prayed and waited for more information.

I had just walked into the house when I received a text from one of the SEAL wives.

Turn on the TV. XNN.

Switching on the TV, I flipped to the cable news channel.

"Again, details are still sketchy," the news anchor said. "But a reliable source within the DoD has confirmed that the casualties are indeed from JSOC."

SEAL Team 6 was a part of JSOC and Drake was the sniper of Fire Team—its most secretive unit.

I hadn't talked to him since our last video call a week ago. Our conversation had been stilted because Drake couldn't talk about his mission. He'd slipped into warrior mode, and not the loving husband he was with me when he was stateside. It was the wrong time to tell him I was pregnant.

I glared at the TV, grabbed the remote, and turned it off. If anyone could survive the odds, it was Drake.

I had faith in him.

He was going to walk through that door at any moment.

I entered our bedroom and picked up the pregnancy test. This week had been a rollercoaster. On Tuesday, I'd come home from my doctor deliriously happy that I was six-weeks pregnant and, twenty-four hours after that, I'd come crashing down into every military wife's nightmare.

I glanced at the clock on the wall. Seven in the morning. I'd just been promoted to senior architect at Stockman and Bose Builders, but I'd have to call in and take another personal day.

I rested a hand on my flat stomach, drawing strength from the life growing inside me. "Your dad is going to be fine. He's a superhero." The stress was driving me insane and it couldn't be good for my pregnancy. My mind desperately sought that time months ago when Drake brought up plans to start a family.

I was sitting beside Drake on the couch, laptop in front of me and absorbed in the modifications to a crucial project. My husband was watching football, but I could feel his gaze on me. In the beginning of our relationship, his frank appraisals made me self-conscious. I would blush to the roots of my hair. Now, it warmed my heart, thinking just how crazy Drake was about me. It scared me sometimes how much I loved him, but I always felt secure that he would always be careful with my heart.

My mouth twitched. "Game boring you?" My eyes stayed focused on the screen, but my belly fluttered with anticipation. We'd been together six years and just a look from him still made my toes curl.

"I was just thinking," he said conversationally, but there was something in his voice that made me look at him. "How happy it would make me to have a daughter who looks exactly like you."

"What are you saying?"

The TV roared with a rousing cheer from the football crowd, but my husband continued to ignore the game. Instead, he picked up the remote, pointed it at the TV, and switched it off. Then he scooted closer and sequestered my laptop, setting it on the coffee table. He did all this without taking his eyes off me.

"SEAL contract is up for renewal," he told me. "I'm not re-enlisting."

"But—"

He raised a finger to my lips, effectively silencing me before sweetly tracing its outline with his thumb. "We've talked about starting a family before. We both agreed when the time is right, I'll resign from the Navy. I'm ready." He took a deep breath. "I hope to God you are. Have my babies, Iza. Give me little girls with their mother's eyes and glorious hair…"

"And if we have boys?" My voice was choked with emotion.

His wide grin told me everything I needed to know.

THE SLAMMING of car doors jolted me out of the sweet memory. I forced my feet to move and walked out of the bedroom. Through the living room windows, I saw two black SUVs. Time stood frozen as I stared at the door.

"Go away," I whispered. "Please, dear God, not this."

The dreaded knock came.

Tears wet my cheeks, and my heart pounded painfully. Still, my body refused to budge.

The doorbell rang, and I came unstuck. Body-shaking tremors tore through me and, before I knew it, I was at the door, throwing it open. Two SEALs in dress blues and two Navymen stood there. I didn't recognize any of them.

"Mrs. Maddox, I'm sorry to inform you…"

"Nooooo!" Their words echoed in a vacuum as my knees and hit the floor. Hands gently clasped my arms.

Soothing voices tried to reach me, but grief kept me locked in a nightmare.

My rage.

"It's not him!" I screamed. "You're wrong. Tell me you're wrong."

The SEAL shook his head. "I'm sorry."

"It's not him," I continued to sob. "Not my Drake."

I didn't know how long I cried.

Much later, details of the massacre trickled in.

Fire Team was gone; their lone survivor was Commander Harrelson. Twenty SEALs killed in action—drawn into a trap.

Many more operators from different JSOC units lost their lives that day.

Eight SEAL wives had become widows.

Twenty-one children had lost their fathers.

Including my unborn child.

chapter two

Four months later

Izabel

I stared at the ceiling.

The sun peeked through the blinds, promising another glorious fall morning, but my world was painted in shades of joyless gray. Every day, it was a chore to get out of bed, to shower, to get to work, and to keep my mind busy, because the alternative was to shrink into myself and disappear into a desolate landscape. That wouldn't do.

Movement in my belly gave me a reason to stay strong. I put my palm reflexively over it, as if it gave me strength.

"Thanks for reminding me, baby girl."

That was the only spark of happiness in a stretch of bleak days. I forced my body to leave the bed.

I ached.

Deep in my heart to the bottom of my soul, I ached, because I missed him desperately. "Why can't you be here, Drake?"

Pain formed a lump in my throat and hot tears pooled in my eyes. A scene replayed every morning since the day my husband was killed.

The phone rang.

Cindy calling.

I sighed. Cindy Lake was my best friend and coworker. She was also the personal assistant of my project manager at Stockman and Bose.

"You're coming in late?" she asked when I answered the phone.

"I think I can make it on time."

There was a slight pause and then, "I know it's hard, Izzy, and you do phenomenal work when you show up, but I heard the boss griping yesterday about your tardiness."

"I'll try harder," I whispered. Though Drake's insurance covered most of my expenses, my job kept me sane. It made me get up each morning. For that alone, I couldn't afford to lose it.

"Did you go to your session yesterday?"

"Yes." I attended group bereavement services besides my private counseling sessions. "I'm not sure it's helping."

"Give it time, Izzy."

That was what everyone told me, but I was beginning to believe it was a lie. The hollowness inside me kept growing each day, threatening to swallow me whole.

"Well, I have to go if I'm going to make it to the office on time." I ended the call and sucked in a ragged breath, fortifying my resolve for the workday ahead. Leaving my bedroom, I passed by the big picture window with a planter situated underneath. Twelve potted orchids—once my pride and joy—now sat shrunken and dead in their clay pots. In my own morbid way, I purposely didn't throw them in the trash can because they reflected the current world I lived in.

I walked into the kitchen, sighing again as I pulled out my breakfast from the fridge. No matter how hard it was to muster an appetite, I made sure I ate properly to nurture the life growing inside me. I was clinging to hope that the last piece I had of Drake would pull me out of this darkness.

Dammit, I was going to be late!

I ditched the basement garage and parked on the street. I hurried out of my car, bumping the door closed with my hip. I beeped the locks and glanced at both sides of the street before I started for my building.

"Watch out!"

I registered a dark blur before the most excruciating pain rammed into me. My body was airborne before the unforgiving pavement stole my breath.

"My baby!" Contractions started almost immediately amidst screams and yells. "Help me…oh, God, please."

I folded over in a fetal position as if it would ease the agony.

And then there was nothing.

. . .

"A BIKE HIT HER…"

"…placental abruption…"

"…too much blood…"

"Need a C-section now!"

I drifted in and out of consciousness. Lights, shadows, and unfamiliar faces hovered over me.

"Drake," I mumbled. "I need Drake."

"I'm here, Iza."

"I want to be with you, but our baby needs me."

"I understand."

"…lungs underdeveloped. Can't survive…"

I AWAKENED to a dimly lit room and a cloak of numbness. A blond head was bowed over folded arms, sleeping at my bedside.

"Cindy," I croaked, reaching out and touching my friend.

Cindy bolted up straight, and the look on her face strangled my heart in fear.

It was then I knew. Even before my friend uttered a single word, I knew.

I lost my baby.

Numbness disappeared, replaced by the agony of having my heart ripped from my chest. Fate couldn't be so cruel a second time to snuff the life growing in my womb.

My mind spurned the terrifying thought.

"No!" I choked. "Tell me I didn't lose her, too."

Cindy's eyes filled with tears and spilled down her cheeks. She gripped my hand. "She was too small." Her lips quavered as she explained, "At twenty-two weeks, her lungs…"

"My fault…"

"No, Izzy, it was the fault of that bike messenger."

We clung to each other in shared sorrow. No other words were spoken for the longest time; the room filled with the heartbreaking wails of a mother who had lost her child.

How can I survive this? Without Drake. And now without our baby, too?

"I need him to be here!" I cried in my friend's arms. "Why can't he be here? I can't go through this alone."

"I'm here, Izzy."

"I need Drake," I sobbed over and over.

It was then I realized that my life in the coming months was going to be a cycle of chilling numbness or gut-wrenching pain.

There was no in-between.

DRAKE

"I'M SORRY, BROTHER."

My chair scraped back as I sprung up, backing away from the screen in disbelief.

"When?" I rasped.

"Yesterday," Hank said solemnly. "A bike messenger took a corner too fast and hit her." He blew out a breath. "She hit the pavement with too much force, caused some complications and severe bleeding. They had to do an emergency C-section."

Hank's words grew muffled as I processed the horror Izabel had gone through—must still be going through.

Losing our daughter…

"… she's banged up, but otherwise okay…"

Rage flared through my veins at his words. "She. Is. Not. Okay," I gritted. "She just lost me…and now…"

Without saying another word and with emotion making it difficult to speak, I pivoted on my heel and exited the comm room, ignoring the pain shooting down my bad leg and the discomfort in my back. I was leaving this place and going home to Izabel. My wife needed me. We would figure out a way to survive the threats against us.

I was stuffing clothes into a duffel when the door to my room opened. Out of the corner of my eye, I made out my teammates, Brick, a ginger-haired former SEAL, and Edmunds, one of Viktor's Guardians.

I ignored them and continued packing, even as the air bristled with my aggression.

"Where are we going?" Brick asked slowly.

"Home," I clipped, muscles coiled, ready to take on my teammates. I zipped the duffel closed and turned to face them squarely, lifting my chin in challenge. "Izabel needs me."

"We heard what happened," Brick said, eyes wary, voice soft. "We're sorry."

I nodded. "I'll catch a flight from Ramstein."

"How do you propose to do that?" Edmunds asked evenly. "You don't exist. Drake Maddox is dead."

"That's bullshit and you know it," I shot back. "A couple of keystrokes and I can be reinstated."

"And how about Fire Team?" Brick challenged. "Remember them?"

I charged my friend and slammed him against the wall.

"What do you think?" I snarled. My head felt like exploding from the force of my anger, not knowing where to direct my fury. "I have nightmares. Every fucking single night, I'm trapped in that cave. I see my brothers blown up. Repeatedly. I hear their screams for help." I let go of Brick's shirt and staggered back. "But it's not real because they didn't even get the chance to scream. They were simply… obliterated." I shuddered. "Sometimes, I wished I had died along with them, but…Izabel."

These past few months, I was a man conflicted.

Duty to avenge my brothers versus my love for my wife.

Guilt that I survived and hope that I would be reunited with my Iza.

Just when I'd accepted that going after the bastards was the right thing to do, the universe threw me a curve ball and all I could see was Izabel's despair.

It was tearing me in half.

"I have to go to her." I turned away from them and resumed shoving the rest of my things into another bag. The hairs on my back prickled as I sensed an imminent threat and, before I could react, something stabbed my neck.

"What the fuck?" I roared, clamping down on Edmunds' wrist at the same time jabbing him in the face.

Cartilage cracked, and blood spattered.

I yanked the still-embedded needle from my neck and squared off against Brick, but they simply watched me.

My vision darkened even as hopeless rage consumed me. "Fuck you both," I slurred, falling against a chair. I tried to remain upright. "Damn you." I was about to pitch forward when someone caught me.

"Sorry, man."

I SPENT days in solitary confinement. A room with no windows and one light bulb. A room used for captured hostiles. No way to tell time. The bastards had taken my watch. I slept on a mattress with no bed frame. There was a toilet and a sink in one corner. Food and water were shoved through an opening in the door. I hadn't fully healed from my injuries, and missing my physical therapy sessions made me hurt like a motherfucker. I massaged my right leg where a muscle spasmed.

I regained consciousness and found myself locked in a room, but I was lucid enough not to cause myself further injury. All I could do was roar and curse. There was an overwhelming urge to hit the wall with my fists, but I had just overcome the tremor in my right hand. If I re-injured it, I could kiss shooting straight goodbye. Endless hours and days passed. In the beginning, I seethed with impotence. But through the war waging inside me, I finally saw clarity by remembering one of the best moments of my life.

. . .

THE NOR'EASTER DUMPED two feet of snow in Ithaca, New York, but even mother nature couldn't stop a determined SEAL. Commercial flights were already grounded, but I got into the city before the worst of the weather hit, hitching a ride with one of my friends who worked for the National Guard. Air travel by Black Hawk was nothing new.

I was holed up in Izabel's tiny studio apartment, the wide windows set against exposed brick walls served as a front-row seat to the winter tempest. The wind howled balefully, and the radiator struggled to keep the dwelling warm, but there was no place I would rather be.

Stirring cocoa into a mug of steaming milk, I walked over to the dining table where Izabel was studying for an exam. She was in the final year of her architectural degree. The last thing she needed was distraction from a boyfriend, but I couldn't help myself.

She needed to be mine.

Izabel glanced up distractedly when I laid down the hot cocoa beside her. Books, notepads, and crumpled paper covered every inch of the surface. She wore her fleece robe over her flannel pajamas, her nose red from the constant sniffles as her body attempted to stay warm.

"Thanks." She smiled before burying her nose back into her textbook.

"That's the least I can do." I sat in the chair beside her, grabbed her hand that wasn't holding a pen, and rubbed it between my palms to help circulation. "Since you don't want me to keep you warm in bed."

Izabel's soft laugh made my chest contract. "I told you not to come up this weekend because I was going to be busy."

"Nothing was keeping me away."

"I see that." She put down her pen and surrendered her other hand to my ministrations. "Oh my God, that feels so good," she groaned as I *massaged her hands between mine. With her eyes closed, I wanted to pepper kisses all over her face.*

Staring at her unusual beauty was a habit I never grew tired of, but more than her physical attributes, it was her inner strength and determination that drew me into her orbit. A heady combination of fire and sass and a whole lotta sweet.

Izabel had stolen my heart and I didn't want it back.

"Iza." My voice was gruff.

Her eyes fluttered open—mesmerizing caramel irises that made words stick in my throat. When a crease formed between her brows, I found my voice and spoke, all words from a prepared speech forgotten.

"Mother nature ruined my plans," I led in. "I'd planned to take you out to a romantic dinner." I glanced outside and grinned ruefully. "That's not happening anytime soon."

Her lips parted and trembled slightly.

"But I couldn't wait, Iza." Not letting go of her hands, I knelt in front of her. Her eyes glistened with unshed tears and she held back the sob that rose to her throat when she realized what I was about to do. "Every time I'm away from you it's as if I'm missing a limb. I can't leave for another mission without worrying someone is going to steal you away from me." At her confused gasp, I added, "I'm an insecure son of a bitch when it comes to you. Can't help it, don't wanna help it, deal with it."

At her annoyed huff, I sighed. "Before I mess this up further." I reached into my pocket and held the ring I'd purchased weeks ago.

"Marry me." Tears spilled down her cheeks and my own heart expanded to the point of exploding. "I'm soul-deep in love with you. I never understood what that meant until you. So marry me, Iza. Make me the happiest damned bastard on the planet."

. . .

THAT MEMORY WAS like a faded photograph, but I never forgot the feeling of the day she said *yes*. I'd never experience that level of happiness with Izabel again until I hunted down the murderers of Fire Team. I loved her with my entire soul, but the core that held my spirit lay in ruins at my feet like the jagged pieces of rocks that buried my brothers.

An eerie calm settled over me as I regained perspective of what needed to be done.

I DIDN'T KNOW how much time had passed when Viktor walked in. I sat up and scowled at the older man. Viktor grabbed the lone chair in the room, flipped it so the back rest was facing me before straddling the seat.

"How are you feeling, Lieutenant?"

"What do you think?"

"I apologize for your accommodations."

"When are you letting me out?"

"Are you still planning on leaving the task force?"

"How's Izabel?" I countered.

Viktor sighed. "She's coping as best as she can."

"I need more than that."

"Your buddy Hank flew out to see her. I assume Izabel knows him?"

I gave a brief nod. "How many days have I been in here?"

"Five."

"You can let me out."

Viktor scrutinized my countenance and his slight smile indicated he liked what he saw.

A stone-cold killer.

chapter **three**

Three years later

Drake

That night's op was the most important one of my life.

I reassembled my automatic rifle. Cleaning my weapons was a way to focus my mind on a mission. The years had transformed me into Viktor's lethal shadow operator.

Task Force Deadly Spear (TFDS) was born when Washington's bureaucracy and politics all but crippled the special operations community, rendering the CIA ineffective and leaving the United States vulnerable to terrorist attacks.

Years of TFDS intelligence work yielded a series of small surgical strikes that chipped at the terrorist network responsible for the biggest loss of life on a single day in special operations history.

Maharib Altanwir was a secretive terrorist organization led by Youssef Hamza—known as the "Warrior" or Maharib. He lost his entire family in Sudan—caught in the crossfire between a terrorist group and operators from Fire Team. I remembered that mission. The terrorists had used civilians as shields. Among them were Hamza's wife and three daughters.

Hamza had a tight inner circle. He never did his own dirty work, but planted chatter in terror networks, manipulating their members into suicide missions through enlightenment propaganda. The day Fire Team was lost, suicide bombers blew themselves up. It took a couple of months for TFDS to figure out that other terrorist networks were being manipulated by a single mastermind.

Youssef Hamza and his Warrior of Enlightenment organization would meet its end that night. Viktor's analysts uncovered the location of Youssef's lair.

After three years, I could finally return to Izabel.

Izabel.

Fuck.

Hank had warned me to avoid social media. He created an account for me, pretending to be an architect whom Iza had met at a convention. Catfishing was a new low, but it had been my link to her. My way of looking in on her. I didn't obsess about it and checked on her maybe once or twice a month. I rarely had downtime anyway. Hank maintained my social media updates, making sure that posts and pictures came from a U.S. location.

About a year ago, Izabel had opened an account on an online dating website. I had lost my shit. That was the one fucking time social media cracked the walls I'd built around my emotions. Hank assured me he'd do everything in his power so Izabel wouldn't find a match. That calmed me down a bit, but my friend had no control when the interest came from a coworker.

A hotshot new architect from Iza's firm had tagged her in a post and she looked…happy.

My heart rolled painfully. I gripped the barrel of the rifle and imagined that punk's neck between my fingers. Surely, Iza couldn't be attracted to that shithead.

I squeezed my eyes shut and replaced the image of Izabel with that of my dead comrades, letting cold fury seep into my veins.

I cleared my mind until one directive remained.
Get Hamza.

———

HARRAN, Turkey
  0200 local time

THE TARMAC BLAZED with lights as our tactical SUVs arrived at the hangar. Outside the structure, two Black Hawks sat with their rotors churning slowly and their engines keyed up in that familiar whine.

We had two assault teams—each with four operators. The mission code was Lightning. I was Lightning One. Brick was Lightning Two and led the second team. Each team had a sniper who would provide elevated cover fire.

My team piled into the waiting choppers. I nodded to a man in a flight suit. "You my gunner?"

"Yes, sir." He needed to verify this shit because when we get dropped into a hot zone, we needed cover fire before our sniper got situated.

On my team was Edmunds; Spike, a former army ranger and sniper; and Rex, an ex-recon Marine who was also our demolitions expert. Our target was forty minutes away in a compound in Al Bab, Syria, that was on the outskirts of Aleppo. I consulted the pilot regarding the drop point. From the latest intel, fast roping wasn't possible, with tangos guarding the compound. The INFIL (infiltration) plan would clear the rooftops of the outbuildings with our fifty-caliber machine gun and drop snipers into place.

As the bird lifted off and accelerated to regular cruising speed, we sat back to get our mind on the mission. We were flying into Syrian airspace without permission. Everyone on both helos knew if we got caught, we would be on our own. Washington would deny our existence.

Our helos flew by deserted wastelands and long stretches of highway, cruising low and completely blacked out as we stealthily approached the destination.

"Three minutes," the pilot announced.

That was a signal for us to check our equipment, weapons, and ammo. Our gunner prepared the fifty cals and rotated the rounds. Our bird dropped almost to the ground before jumping over the barrier surrounding the compound.

In the span of several heartbeats, the night lit up with muzzle flashes. The team was jostled around as the pilot outmaneuvered the tracer assault. Then the bird banked left so our gunner could pave the way for insertion.

The hostiles retreated as the machine gun tore through the courtyard, cutting some of them in half before rising to the tallest structure and neutralizing the guards there as well. Spike dropped to the rooftop to assume sniper duties.

"Eagle in position," Spike reported.

"Copy that," Brick replied. "Dropping our package as well." Lightning Two and his team were breaching the same building but from the rear entrance. This was to mitigate any enemy escape, especially our primary target.

Our helo returned to the courtyard, now empty of tangos, but the muzzle flashes continued from inside our target—a two-story concrete structure. Our gunner and Spike provided cover fire as we jumped to the ground.

I went first, took a knee, and sighted through my rifle as my team moved ahead. As the bird lifted off, I joined my men, and we shuffled toward our target in combat stance.

Spike made sure our path was clear and kept the hostiles from firing.

Mostly.

We reached the door and Rex immediately set the breaching charge.

As the entrance exploded, I tossed in a flash-bang grenade.

I tapped Edmunds. He forged ahead.

"Clear left," he yelled.

Rex followed. "Clear right!"

I followed down the center and became the first man in our three-man stack. Eyes behind my rifle's sight, I swept from room to room. The second room on our right yielded a huddle of women and children.

"Got this. Go!" Edmunds stayed behind to guard them while Rex and I continued on.

We reached a corner-fed room that was between two hallways. Spying Brick coming from the opposite hallway, the other team lead nodded. "Go ahead, One."

I keyed my mic twice and then took a big step to balance my pivot into the room just as Rex swept in behind me. "Clear."

Before us were stairs leading to the second floor. I was sure the hostiles were lying in wait, ready to spray us with bullets but, from my experience, they were too eager and jumpy. The house was in total darkness and everything was lit up only by our night vision goggles. Leading by the dot from my scope, I sighted movement and squeezed off two shots just as gunfire erupted down the steps. A man in a white robe fell on the landing. Sporadic fire met me at the top of the steps, but the hostiles were shooting blindly. Rex and I quickly got rid of two more.

The first room at the top of the steps was clear but was laden with file cabinets and computers. One of Brick's men stayed behind to collect hard drives and disks.

With a third room cleared, that left the last one at the end of the hallway. This was going to be—

Gunshots blasted holes through the door. A force slammed into me and knocked me to my ass. A fiery arc swept above me. Someone dragged my dead weight into the last room we cleared.

"Son of a bitch," I hissed. Chest on fire, I checked my vest and exhaled a painful breath.

"You all right?" Brick asked.

"Yeah. SAPI plate stopped the fucking round," I choked.

"Looks like Youssef is making a last stand." Brick gave me a hand up.

"Sounds good to me," I muttered.

Rex entered the room. "Got an SED on the door."

Through the throbbing of my chest, I grinned. I loved our toys. Sticky Explosive Device was a bomb that could attach to any surface. It was our last resort if the tango had no plans of surrendering because of the destruction it could cause. I wanted Youssef dead and not to waste another molecule of oxygen on the bastard who'd killed my brothers.

"Light him up."

I STARED at the mangled body of the man who'd eluded capture for so long. If Youssef Hamza hadn't died from the blast wave, he would have bled out from the tear to his femoral artery. A piece of the door had turned into a deadly spear and pierced Hamza in his thigh and sliced through the critical vessel if the massive pool of blood under him was anything to go by.

Brick received confirmation from our analyst that the transmitted image was indeed the Maharib Altanwir mastermind.

His end was fatalistic, poetic justice.

For me, it was a chance for my life to move forward. The weight in my chest, the need to avenge my fallen brothers had finally lifted as a sense of freedom took hold. The shackles of Deadly Spear fell off and I could look to a future again.

A future with Izabel.

RAMSTEIN-MIESENBACH, Germany
1800 local time

"So, any idea what you're going to do after this?"

Brick's question broke through my thoughts. Now that Youssef Hamza was dead and his organization was in tatters, I was anxious to reintegrate into society. But getting back to Izabel wouldn't be as easy as I first thought. Though she may come to understand why I faked my death, she wouldn't have agreed to that plan if she'd had a say in it. She would have gone on the run with me. Even if I were crippled and with Hamza breathing down our necks, she would have stood by my side. No, she'd be furious if she found out the truth.

I'd broken her trust. Gaining it back would be the toughest fight of my life.

"Go home. Get back to my wife." I wanted to snort because I had no fucking clue how to approach her.

"Are you joining the SEALs again?"

"No. I had planned on quitting. The day everything went to hell...that was supposed to be my last mission." Pain stabbed my chest as I remembered the baby we lost.

"Does that mean I don't get to call you Dave anymore?"

Dave Morgan had been my identity. I made myself respond to both names because I'd always intended to return as Drake Maddox.

"You can call me whatever, Brick."

"I'll miss your ugly mug," the ginger-haired operator said.

The door opened and the rest of the crew filed in. Viktor brought up the rear with his data analyst, Tim. The man was a whiz with computers, just like Hank.

"Tim analyzed some of the information collected from Hamza's compound and we believe we'll be able to identify who leaked the plans of the JSOC operation to the various terror networks."

"Weren't you certain it was someone from the administration?" Brick asked.

"We need hard evidence before accusing a high-ranking official of treason."

I smiled grimly. "Didn't think that ever stopped you before."

Viktor smirked. "I've turned over a new leaf."

Snorts and varying degrees of laughter made the rounds in the room. Everyone knew Viktor didn't stick to protocol and didn't give a damn who he'd crossed. I had a suspicion he had dirt on everyone, including the President. This was what made the man and his company—Artemis Guardians Services (AGS)—lethal. They had special ops skills, brains, and international connections that made them virtually unstoppable. Despite my initial resistance to working for the man, much of what I'd learned under Viktor opened my eyes to a world where politics had no control over what was needed to get things done.

"The Director is very pleased with the information we've recovered," Viktor said. "He's thinking of expanding the task force objectives to go after other terrorists organizations."

I froze. "I'm out."

"We haven't finished the mission, *Morgan*."

"It's *Maddox*."

Viktor snorted. "Until we find out who leaked intel of classified military ops to Hamza, our mission is *not* over."

"Understood. But that sounds like the work of an analyst and a spook, not people with my skill set." I nodded to Brick and the other men on the team.

Viktor smiled faintly. "Haven't you learned what it means to be a spy after three years?"

I emitted a disgruntled sound. There were times when I'd donned a tuxedo for some function to gain information. Part of the training that was hammered into me while I recovered from my injuries was learning the craft of espionage.

"Your documents." Viktor tipped his chin at Tim, who proceeded to hand out Manila envelopes to a couple of us. A flash drive, a passport, and a birth certificate fell out. A weight pressed down on my chest as I ran my thumb over my name and the picture on the passport. I couldn't wait to shed the Dave Morgan skin and return to who I once was, but Viktor was right. The job wasn't done. Whether I had more to offer remained to be seen.

"If the traitor is within the administration, this might be a job for the DoJ and FBI," I pointed out. "We're pushing our jurisdiction too far."

I winced when the words fell out of my mouth. It sounded hypocritical and judging from the glimmer in

Viktor's eyes and the suppressed cough from Brick, they thought the same. Our team had broken so many laws in other countries, I had lost count. In the beginning, I had problems adjusting to that mindset after being restricted by the rules of engagement the JSOC had instilled into their operators. But with Task Force Deadly Spear, the rules had not only been broken, they'd been obliterated.

There was only one rule: *Don't get caught.*

"Fuck," I muttered.

"Exactly," Viktor murmured. "We're ghosts, remember?" A cautionary tone in the man's voice made me look up.

"Use your alias when you enter U.S. soil." He turned to me. "I can't stop you from seeing Izabel—"

"Damn right," I growled.

Viktor chuckled. "Can't say I envy your situation. Have you figured out how to approach her yet?"

"Not really." Somehow, driving up to the front of the house, hoping she'd fly down the steps and jump into my arms was wishful thinking.

"If she refuses to speak to you, we can always kidnap her and keep her in the AGS bunker until she talks to you."

My eyes narrowed. "There will be no kidnapping."

"You sure about that, Maddox?"

Everyone busted out laughing, and I couldn't stop from grinning.

"I'll let you know."

chapter
four

Izabel

"You're not backing out from that date," I heard Cindy say through my phone speaker. She was now my PA after I had been promoted to project manager.

Throwing myself into my job helped me through the grief, but I wouldn't have made it without Cindy, especially when I lost my baby a mere four months after Drake's death.

Pain dug into my chest.

Tears sprung to my eyes.

Would there ever come a time when their loss wouldn't hurt? That was why I'd finally agreed to go on an actual date and not one that was work-related. Maybe falling in love with someone else was the answer. Counseling sessions, group therapy, and the passage of time had dulled the ache, but there were still days of crippling pain.

"I'm not backing out. Kyle's great." He was the new architect at the firm and had been my date at the company gala last week. I hadn't experienced belly flutters the way I had with Drake, but I had accepted that my husband was the love of my life. My soul mate. But like my grief counselor said, the heart had room to love more than one person, and it didn't mean I was replacing Drake.

There was no replacing Drake.

But I had to move on somehow. Because this gaping emptiness? It had gone on for too long and I was barely existing outside my job.

A light sigh of relief whooshed at the other end of the line. "Good. I don't know why you couldn't find a match on RightSpark."

It had been Cindy who opened an account for me on the online dating website saying she'd had much success there.

"Online dating doesn't work for everyone. Just because it worked for you, it doesn't mean it'd work for me. And, for the love of God, don't go opening accounts for me on all these websites."

A hearty laugh came over the phone. "I just hate to see a beautiful woman like you remain single for the rest of your life. I'm sure your husband would've wanted you to find someone else and be happy."

I wasn't sure that was a true statement. Drake was over-the-top possessive. I imagined even in death he wouldn't be willing for another man to have me. The corners of my lips tipped into a small smile.

"Didn't you meet Drake in school?" Cindy asked suddenly.

"I was in my last year of grad school," I replied. "I was the nerdy girl my classmates dragged to a bar. At twenty-six, I'd never had a serious boyfriend."

"I can't believe that."

"I had a scholarship at an Ivy League university and I wasn't going to mess that up by getting distracted."

"And then Drake swept you off your feet," Cindy gushed.

I laughed. "You could say that." Contrary to what people believed, SEALs were a low-key bunch when they were out in public. I wasn't even aware of their group at the noisy honky-tonk bar and hadn't known that Drake had already singled me out from all the women in the establishment. He startled me when I exited the ladies' room and was about to attack him with pepper spray. He disarmed me easily and somehow managed to charm me enough to leave the bar with him. We ended up talking for hours in his pickup and had breakfast at a diner at two in the morning. He was in the area because one of his buddies was from Ithaca and was getting married.

"He gave me the best six years of my life." My voice cracked.

"Shit, honey, the last thing I want to do is set you back," Cindy said.

"I'm okay." And I was determined to move on, *dammit*.

"Have you heard from Marcus?" she asked.

I winced at the mention of Drake's former commander. If there was someone whose loss was beyond catastrophic, it was Marcus Harrelson. To have lost his entire team and his family within days had proven too much for him to bear. He'd drowned his sorrows in a bottle and gotten addicted to painkillers. He got kicked out of the Teams. I'd visited him every few weeks after he'd come back from rehab.

"Yes. A couple of days ago."

"Does he look better?"

"Yes. I think this time rehab will stick. He seems more focused at work." I had gotten Marcus a job with the firm's security department. With Marcus's background and the circumstances of his past, our boss was willing to overlook his one transgression of showing up drunk at work. But rehab had been a part of the deal.

"I feel so bad for him," Cindy mumbled. My assistant had a soft spot for Marcus. "I wish Veteran's Affairs would devote more budget to mental health."

"Good luck with that," I muttered. I wasn't much into politics but had heard enough from Drake about every slash in budget for military veterans.

"Maybe I should make him a casserole this weekend," she said.

"Cindy," I warned. "Leave the man alone. He's fine."

"Well, I'll let you go so you can get ready."

When our call ended, my anticipation for the date soured a little. I had an hour and a half before Kyle picked me up at seven. I had time to psyche myself back into looking forward to dinner instead of dreading it.

I found my happiness nine years ago. Drake pursued me relentlessly between deployments. We video chatted often when he was down range. He'd scheduled deliveries of flowers and chocolates when he wasn't around so I'd always think of him. And when he returned, he tried as much as possible to see me, flying up to New York from Virginia Beach, even when it was simply to hang around my apartment while I studied for my finals. Within eight months of knowing each other, we got married. I moved to Virginia Beach and interned with Stockman and Bose Builders and had stayed in the area since.

Three months before that fated mission, Drake mentioned building a house. He had a sizable inheritance from his grandmother's side. He had no close family to take care of since his parents died when he was young. He was quitting the SEALs and had contacts in the private security business who were offering good money at more than triple his salary as a SEAL.

As if in a trance, I walked over to my home office and pulled out the bottom drawer of the stacking flat-file cabinet. I gently lifted the sheets of vellum paper. The beautiful two-story house I'd lovingly drawn was smeared in several places. I didn't care if more tears fell and splattered the ink on the design to the point of ruin.

This house would never be built.

"You're so beautiful tonight."

I lifted the wineglass and sipped, uncertain how to respond to Kyle's compliment except, "Thank you." What he didn't know was I spent fifteen minutes with a cold compress to my swollen eyes after my bout of ugly crying.

"Do I make you uncomfortable?" Kyle asked gently.

"I haven't been on a date for years. Ah…it's a bit awkward."

"Fair enough." His blue eyes crinkled at the corners. "I hope you're enjoying your dinner at least."

We were at a French restaurant. He'd asked me about my favorite food. Honestly, it would be Drake's grilled steaks—his MadDog special—but that was hardly an appropriate answer, so I answered the next best thing…anything cooked with a lot of butter. I wasn't picky. I'd known what it was like to go without, having almost become homeless in my teens when my mother could not work because of an injury.

"Oh, yes." To prove my point, I forked a delicate morsel of buttered fish into my mouth. The track of Kyle's eyes from my plate to my mouth almost made me choke, especially when I saw them spark with desire.

Drake often teased me about how just the sight of my bow-shaped lips made him hard.

I mentally berated myself for thinking of my dead husband while on a date with another man. Feeling rebellious at my inability to move on, I shot Kyle a sultry gaze. "Do you want to try my dish?"

Startled, color rushed up his cheeks. He was really handsome in that all-American golden-boy way. As opposed to Drake's dark hair and rugged build, Kyle had a lean runner's frame. And…there I went comparing the two again.

"Sure," Kyle replied and shot me a goofy grin.

I cringed at the sound of my nervous giggle, but forced myself to dutifully lift a piece of fish and sweetly offered it to him to try. I inhaled deeply and exhaled slowly as I relaxed into conversation and our meal. It helped that we could talk about architectural trends and our projects.

"Congratulations on convincing the board to offer our services for free to the Solace affordable-housing project," Kyle said.

"It wasn't my accomplishment alone. My team helped, and so did the Solace Foundation."

"Yes, but you spearheaded the program. You should be proud of what you've done."

"It's the right thing to do," I said. "When my mother broke her wrist and couldn't work at the salon, we couldn't afford our mortgage and almost ended up on the streets."

"But it didn't happen, right?" Kyle frowned.

"No. Ma had an ace in her pocket," I sighed. "She had to swallow a lot of her pride, but she got our heads above water. Still, I'll never forget what that felt like." Eating canned food for days, selling our television. My mother almost sold her treasured scissors—a hairstylist's lifeblood.

"I'm confused. You did your undergrad and masters at Cornell."

"I had a scholarship." I smiled. "And Ma…"

"The ace in her pocket?" Kyle raised a brow.

"Nothing devious," I replied. "Let's just say I was given a fair chance to qualify. Hey, this is our first date. You're not expecting me to tell you my life story, are you?"

Kyle grinned sheepishly and changed the subject.

After we ordered dessert, my gaze wandered around the restaurant. That was when I noticed a man at the corner of the nickel-plated bar.

"Kyle?"

"Yes, my sweet?"

The endearment made me pause, but I decided to roll with it. "I see a friend at the bar. Do you mind if I say hello?"

"Not at all," Kyle replied as his gaze automatically pulled to the bar. "Go ahead."

I pushed back from my chair and got up. I approached the man at the bar steadily and with purpose.

Hank was facing the dining room and shot me his shit-eating grin.

"What are you doing here?"

"No hello?" Hank came forward and gave me a hug. He'd been a buddy of Drake's and flew in to be with me after that heartbreaking day. "I'm visiting my SEAL buddies."

"And yet you're at a French bistro hanging out alone?"

Hank blew out a breath. "I worry about you, sweetheart."

I rolled my eyes. "I'm a thirty-five-year-old woman and you're treating me like I'm on my first date with a wolf in sheep's clothing."

Hank looked past my shoulder at Kyle. "He looks like a good guy."

I glanced at my date who was watching us curiously. "Kyle *is* a good guy." I leaned in closer. "And don't you dare run a whole background check on him."

As far as I knew, Hank Bristow worked in intelligence. I wasn't exactly sure, but he seemed to know things and showed up when I needed him. I didn't even question how he did it. Drake had been tight-lipped about what his friend did, but I could only surmise that it was a black ops team.

When he didn't reply, I narrowed my eyes. "You already did."

He shrugged.

"I'm trying to move on," I whispered.

"Shit, I'm sorry," Hank muttered and put an arm around me. "I really was in town to meet up with the guys, but I thought I'd check up on you." He gave me a squeeze. "Go back and enjoy your evening with Romeo."

I gave a small snort of laughter. Hank had a way of making an awkward moment turn around.

"We need to catch up," I told him.

"I'd love to, but I'm on a tight schedule."

"Bummer," I mumbled.

After giving him another hug, I made my way back to the table.

"Friend of your husband?" Kyle asked when I sat down.

"Sort of," I evaded. After what had happened to Drake's team, I'd been thinking twice about pointing out a SEAL. In his drunken ramblings, Marcus Harrelson insisted that there was a cover-up in his wife and kids' deaths. Rumors abounded that it was a hit by the same terrorist who masterminded the massacre of Fire Team. But because the Navy refused to spend money on protecting the remaining SEAL widows, they didn't investigate further. No sense discovering a problem they didn't plan to fix.

Our server returned with dessert. I had ordered a lavender crème brûlée while Kyle ordered a chocolate ganache layered bar.

"That looks scrumptious," I remarked at the multilayered chocolate extravaganza.

Kyle chuckled. "Do I detect regret in your tone?"

I cracked the sugary shell of the custard and scooped a creamy spoonful into my mouth. "Hmm…this is good, but I bet yours is better."

His eyes twinkled. "Do you want to exchange?"

My eyes widened. "You'd do that?"

His chuckle deepened, and the walls around my heart cracked as laughter bubbled up my throat.

This was good. Laughter was good.

"It's just dessert, Izabel." Kyle stopped laughing and grinned.

"I mean, lavender crème brûlée isn't exactly something I thought a man would be caught ordering."

"Izabel Maddox." Kyle's voice held a tinge of mock censure. "Do I detect some form of sexist remark from your last statement?"

"Well, have a taste." I held out my spoon.

He screwed up his face. "Uh, no."

"See?" I laughed harder.

"What I meant was—you can have mine and I can order another one."

"Well, I don't want to waste food," I replied pertly and dipped into my crème brûlée again as if to emphasize a point.

Kyle dug into the tempting layers of sinful chocolate and then held it out to me. "Well, would you settle for a bite?"

I smiled impishly. "I would love to."

When Kyle took me home, I marveled at how differently I felt before and after the date. It had been cathartic to laugh and flirt again with a man. Kyle was good company, charming, and he wisely didn't pry into my past with Drake. I'd been having such a wonderful time with him during dessert that I didn't notice Hank leaving. Of course, being a former SEAL, he was stealthy that way.

As Kyle's Porsche pulled up my driveway, I turned to face him. "Thank you for a lovely dinner."

His face was shadowed, but I could feel the heat in his eyes. My breathing stuttered nervously when he leaned in closer until our faces were inches apart.

"I'm going to kiss you," he murmured. "Okay?"

I gulped and nodded.

The first press of his mouth felt totally wrong. I opened my mouth to protest, but Kyle took that as an invitation to delve deeper. His tongue swept into my mouth and he pulled me closer. His kiss was gentle and coaxing, making me want to explore and give in to the moment. His hand slid lower to my hip before settling on top of a thigh, just at the hem of my skirt. Kyle's breathing grew ragged and, although a spark had started low in my belly, I had to stop this.

A car alarm went off in the neighborhood and we both jumped back into our seats.

I ran awkward fingers through my hair. "Um..."

Kyle gave a self-deprecating chuckle. "I'll walk you to the door."

I nodded, relieved to get out of the car.

He waited until I rounded the front of his vehicle and held out his hand. I had no choice but to take it. He tugged me close and together we walked up the pathway.

"I hate to see this evening end," Kyle said as we turned toward each other at the door. The car alarm in the neighborhood was still blaring. "I really like you, Izabel. I know I should wait a couple of days before I call you and ask you for another date, but why waste time?"

"Are you asking me on another date?"

"Would Wednesday be too soon?"

"I don't think so."

"Let's discuss details at the office." He glanced around the neighborhood, a look of irritation crossing his face. "Someone needs to take care of that alarm."

I unlocked the door and pushed it open. "I agree. So," I said, peering up at him. "See you at the office?"

He paused as if wanting to say something, but changed his mind and lowered his head to press a chaste kiss on my lips. "Until Monday then."

Seconds after I closed the door and stepped into the foyer, the annoying car alarm stopped.

Thank God for that.

chapter
five

Izabel

I woke before the sun came up. The relative success of my date with Kyle gave me hope I could finally find happiness again. It might not be with Kyle; it might be with someone else. But this weekend would be about starting over—beginning by getting rid of Drake's things.

When I'd sold our house, I hadn't given away his stuff. I couldn't bring myself to part with pieces of him. His gun safe was in my office. The guns were an extension of Drake. He took utmost care of every single one of them.

Some of Drake's work tools I'd given to Hank. Others I'd given to Marcus.

Drake's commander needed help more than I did. I'd tried dragging him to some grief counseling sessions, but it wasn't only grief that was eating at Marcus. Guilt was involved, too. If only he could talk to someone.

I headed to the attic and stood at the entrance with a feeling like I was about to enter a mausoleum. Sighing, I flicked on the switch, illuminating the room in a ghastly incandescent glow. The smell of stale air, mildew, and old books permeated the space. Boxes labeled *clothes, garage,* and *library* were stacked on top of each other.

I walked over to the window and stared outside. The first rays of the sun peeked through the horizon. It was a bit late to start my morning run, but I'd wanted to wait for more sunlight. The cold air passing over the warm waters of the James River created foggy mornings. I loved running at this time of the year and I'd better get started, because it was going to be a long day. Taking one long look at the boxes, I hardened my resolve that they would be taken care of later.

Definitely today.

By the time I reached the kitchen, the pot of coffee was ready. I poured myself a cup and checked emails and messages.

Fully caffeinated, I changed into running gear and put on my reflectors. It was a cool forty-nine degrees, but I'd warm up after the first mile. The fog was coming in low and the sun's golden rays fighting to break through increased my excitement. It was going to be a gorgeous morning with the patches of fog hovering over the wetlands along the trail behind my house. I was looking forward to the serene view of the sunrise on the arch bridge over the James River.

I picked a playlist and started with a brisk jog, waving to my neighbor, who'd just come off the trail. There were several routes around the park, and since I planned to run five miles today, I'd probably do two passes by the river, where the bridge allowed me to cross over the water to make a loop. I reached the bridge and observed the foggy scenery. The park was unusually empty this Saturday morning.

Movement in my peripheral vision made me turn. The contour of a man broke through the swirling fog rising from under the bridge. An achingly familiar form clad in track pants and a hoodie that shadowed the top half of his face. A thick beard hid the rest. I forced myself to look away. My heart edged up my throat. No, it was because I was thinking about him. For months after Drake was killed, I saw him everywhere. I couldn't go back to that again. Limbo. Barely existing. Sucked out of joy and wishing I'd died along with him.

My breathing quickened and it had nothing to do with the run. The burning despair in my heart switched to alarm when the man didn't pass behind me but, instead, stopped a couple of feet away on my right.

He was looking at the sunrise same as I was.

"Beautiful, isn't it?" the man's gravelly voice reached me.

That voice.

But what triggered my fight or flight had nothing to do with Drake, but my survival instinct due to the overwhelmingly lethal vibe exuded by this stranger. Goose bumps raced across the top of my shoulders and crawled up my scalp. I slanted my gaze to him, keeping my face forward while my hand slowly rested on the pepper spray, thankful I always carried it on my runner's belt. The park was generally safe, but one couldn't be too sure, and neither was I letting any sicko frighten me into avoiding the one activity that gave me peace.

"Baby, you attack me with that pepper spray, I guarantee we won't be spending time talking in the pickup."

I gasped. All thoughts of survival disintegrating as I spun to face the stranger.

The man dragged the hood from his face.

Drake.

He looked a lot like Drake. Broader in shoulders, arms a bit more muscular. I'd seen my husband with a beard, but never one this long. And yet the eyes, the slash of brows, and the slightly crooked nose were unmistakably Drake's.

"Iza..."

My mouth fell open, but shock prevented any words from forming. Thoughts clashed in my head.

Is this a dream?

A sick joke?

Am I losing my mind?

None of this could be real, and yet he uttered my name in the special way Drake did.

In the only way that had ever touched my soul.

He was a magnet drawing me in and I stumbled forward, body shaking, chest heaving, lifting a trembling hand and wanting to touch his face.

"Drake?" I whispered the name full of hope, yet disbelief, still struggling to make sense of the man before me.

A flash of white teeth. His oh-so-familiar smile.

My legs buckled, but before I hit the wooden planks, strong arms swooped around me.

They held me up as I was crushed against a chest. I sobbed—my body not knowing whether to breathe or cry. My mind not knowing how to process thoughts spiraling in a chaotic trajectory, trying to find logic amidst the soothing words murmured against my ear.

"I missed you, Iza. God, how I missed you."

I froze.

He *missed* me?

I went to hell when he died.

Fury, rejection, and betrayal coalesced and squashed the yearnings of my heart. I struggled to get out of his embrace.

"Let me go!" I screamed when he refused to comply.

"Let me go!" I repeated, almost hysterical.

His arms unlocked and I staggered back. "You missed me?" I was panting hard, glaring at the stranger who claimed to be my husband. Well, he could be the stand-in for anger, so explosive that words couldn't even define the agony I went through in the last three years.

If all "ghost Drake" could say was he missed me, then fuck him.

"I stood in that airfield waiting for the plane to bring my husband home. I wept over your flag-draped casket," I inhaled raggedly. His face blurring as the onslaught of tears streamed down my cheeks. "I buried you. I mourned you, Drake, but that's what I signed up for when I married a SEAL, knowing that could happen to us. But this…" I waved my arm up and down in front of me. "I didn't sign up for this. For three years of living hell believing I'd lost the love of my life…"

My words trailed off because logic dictated if this was Drake, then I'd been lied to.

He visibly flinched as he took a step forward. "I can explain, Iza."

I laughed. A scornful laugh, borne out of pain. Everything inside me rebelled against this version of Drake. Because even if this man was Drake, he was not my husband. Not anymore.

"Oh, I'm sure you can," I said between bouts of wracking sobs. I backed away from him because my heart was shattering all over again. "But I don't know if I can forgive you."

I ran.

―――――

Drake

Fuck!

Her anguish hit me like a wave slamming my body against a jagged rock. The devastation of her words sent me reeling, realization dawning on me that I was going to have the fight of my life on my hands. In the past three years, I had imagined our reunion so many times, but damn, was I way off point.

Izabel disappeared into the mist. I had been the envy of my teammates, especially the married ones.

Izabel accepted my sudden deployments as my duty. She never complained.

Missed anniversaries.

Leaving her birthday party because I got called in.

Missed Christmases.

Did I see disappointment in her eyes? Sure I did, but she knew what she signed up for.

I didn't sign up for this.

Her words echoed in my ears. Panic sent me running after her. She was racing through the trails as if the devil himself were after her.

In this case, I was the devil.

I slowed my pace, gave her a twenty-foot distance, but that was all the space she was getting. We'd lost three years and, though it had been entirely my decision that put us in this situation, I couldn't say I wouldn't have made the same choice.

Where Izabel lived.

I can live in a world where she hates me, but I can't live in a world where she doesn't exist.

As we neared her house, a spark of resentment ignited inside me. We had a home. She sold it. Now she was living in a house where there were no memories of us. The first pinprick of fear stabbed my chest that my faked death had broken us beyond repair.

But she left the door open.

Did that mean she was willing to talk? I was prepared to camp out on her steps until she talked to me.

I went up the steps, stopped, massaged the area over my diaphragm, feeling like I had an oncoming heartburn. Venting an exhalation, I moved through the open door, closing it quietly behind me.

Izabel was pacing in front of the table between the kitchen and the living room. She stopped when she saw me enter and speared me a glare before crossing her arms over her chest. That was her defensive posture. The area around her eyes was splotchy and her nose was red. I fought against the instinct to hug and kiss her, but unlike me, who had three years of pent-up longing to return to my wife, she had three years of trying to move on from me.

"Tell me, Drake. Did you think you could simply waltz back into my life after three years? Three years of me thinking you were dead?"

"I never believed it would be easy, Izabel."

"You died. What if I'd moved on?"

"Have you?" I challenged.

"Not yet."

My eyes narrowed. "And you won't."

"You think you can stop me?" she taunted. "You have no hold over me. I have your death certificate." Her face crumpled in confusion and I really, really wanted to kiss those lines away. "So, if you're dead on paper, who are you now?"

That was my Izabel. She was quick to pick up the chink in my story.

"A man called Dave Morgan, but not for long. I prefer being Drake Maddox."

She began pacing again and I could do nothing more but clench my fists at my sides while she processed this information.

"So *technically* you're still this Dave Morgan."

"Yes."

"I just can't wrap my mind around it," Izabel said. "And you didn't answer my question. What if I'd moved on and had gotten married?"

"That wasn't going to happen," I grated. Just the thought of her married to another man was turning me feral. "Hank was watching you for me."

Her eyes widened in understanding. "You knew I was on a date last night?"

"Yes." Hank assured me I didn't have to storm into the restaurant and give Izabel the shock of her life in public, but he couldn't do anything when I insisted on making sure that Izabel didn't sleep with Kyle. I staked out the restaurant from the parking lot and followed them home.

She squinted. "The car alarm."

I nodded, unrepentant. At all.

Her face flamed red as she stared up at the ceiling and then back at me. "Unbelievable."

"Aren't you gonna ask why I faked my death?"

Izabel shook her head. "No." Her shoulders hunched. "I know it's a good reason. I know you thought it was the right decision at that time, but I don't want to hear it yet." Tears filled her eyes again. "I don't want to hear the reason that had me wishing I'd died too."

"Izabel—"

"But I had to be strong because I was pregnant." She watched me closely and whatever she saw on my face made her add, "You knew."

Crippling pain at the loss resurfaced, and all I could do was nod.

"I lost her."

I strained to hear her, but the haunted look on her face said it all. My death and losing the baby had destroyed the woman I loved. To what extent, it was hard to tell. But I couldn't stand not holding her and reached for her, but she shied away. Her entire stance screamed, *"Do not touch me!"*

"Three years." She scrutinized my face, lingering on my

beard, her lips parting when it rested on the scars at my neck that disappeared under the beard. "You're different."

"You always liked me with a beard." I grinned.

"I'm not sure we're the same people."

My smile fell. I promised myself that I would be patient with her, but fuck if it was easier thought than done.

"It's a good thing you came back today." Her back appeared stiff and her expression wasn't exactly as welcoming as her words. "I woke up this morning determined that I was moving on."

"With whom? Kyle?" I spat.

"You've been spying on me this whole time," she snapped. "My life was hell, and you were spectating? And yes, I was hoping to move on. Not necessarily with Kyle, but with my life."

"Some kind of homecoming you have for me, baby." I sneered. Jealousy surged. Patience forgotten.

Izabel raised her hands in surrender. She looked so exhausted. Overwhelmed. The bossy husband in me wanted to take over, but I scrounged back some of my self-control.

"Sorry," I muttered.

"I need to wrap my mind around this," she said. "Before we say things we'll regret." She gave me her back. "Your things are in the attic. Your guns are in the safe in my office. There's a hotel—"

"I'm not staying in some damn hotel. I'm staying right here."

Her shoulders rose and deflated. "I'll fix up the guest room."

She walked away without looking back.

I stood in the middle of the room with a strong desire to smash something in the unfamiliar surroundings my wife called home. It wasn't the reunion I envisioned. Sure, I expected tears. Sure, I expected her anger. I expected Izabel pounding on my chest, railing at me for my decision. But I'd grab her face and kiss her tears away.

I didn't expect this automaton she'd become. I fished my phone out and swiped a number.

The phone rang twice.

"Didn't go well?"

Hank's statement grated on my nerves. The last thing I needed was my friend to say *I told you so*.

"She's not happy."

"You knew this would happen. This is Izabel we're talking about."

"I can fix this. She let me in the house at least."

"That's good."

"I destroyed her trust." My voice grew hoarse.

"Listen, man, we knew you'd have a fight on your hands. The divorce rate among SEALs is ninety-five percent and yet both of you had a great marriage."

"Until I betrayed our vows."

Hank sighed. "Yeah, well, 'for better or worse' and 'until death do us part' hardly apply in this situation."

I grunted. "She's alive. That's all that matters. Looks like I'll have to grovel."

Hank chuckled. "Wish I was there to see it."

"I hope Viktor figures out who our leak is. I can't wait to get out of the shadows."

"You think you'll be running into someone you know in Virginia Beach?"

"I'll worry about that when the time comes, but I wasn't waiting another moment to see Izabel." Especially with another man sniffing around.

"Shit, Izabel is calling my phone. Later," Hank muttered and hung up.

I stared at my phone, and then up the stairs where my wife had disappeared.

chapter
six

Izabel

I didn't know how my legs managed to scale the stairs. Fueled by adrenaline, I supposed. By anger. I was so, so angry. I entered my bedroom and shut the door. Then I leaned against it, letting gravity take me to the floor as whatever strength I had finally deserted me.

Two fierce and opposing emotions drained the strength from my body.

Elation that Drake was alive.

White-hot fury at his betrayal and what he had done to our marriage.

The agony in my chest bled with the pain of a reopened wound.

And yet guilt ate at me.

The scars on his neck…my fingers wanted to touch them.

A part of me that loved my husband wanted to ask what had happened.

But he died, a resentful voice whispered.

Tired of the battle inside me, I pushed up from the floor and called Hank.

My phone rang a few times before he answered. There was no mistaking the hesitation in his voice.

"Izabel."

"You knew."

"I knew."

Silence.

And then, "Is that all you're going to say?" I choked. "You, of all people, knew how much I suffered."

"I'm sorry, Izzy," Hank whispered. "But Drake had no choice. Neither did I. If we broke the agreement with the person who recruited him, I'd lose access to him. And if Drake's identity was compromised, it would—and still may—put you in immediate danger."

"Was I in danger?"

"You need to hear the story from him."

Dread curled in my gut. "Commander Harrelson's family?"

"I'm not at liberty to say."

Weariness tugged on my already-frayed nerves. As a SEAL wife, I understood my husband kept secrets from me, even those that could directly affect me. My reaction to Drake's return suddenly made sense. "I don't know if I can go through this again."

"I don't think Drake's gonna disappear for another three years." There was lightness in his tone.

"That's not what I meant. I don't think I have it in me to be a SEAL wife anymore." I wanted to move on with a safe guy. The man who'd returned to me was far from the definition of safe.

At Hank's muffled curse, I continued, "I think—"

"Izabel," Hank cut in. "Your husband is in your house. Talk to him."

There was a finality in his words. He wasn't going to give me the answers I needed.

"Okay."

"Good girl."

"I'm not promising to be reasonable," I added tartly.

I could almost see Hank's shit-eating grin on the other end of the line. "Give him hell."

A burst of laughter broke through the tightness in my chest. I ended the call and stared at the closed door. Beyond it were the answers I sought.

There were three bedrooms in the house. I wished I picked a house with a first-floor bedroom. I had no choice but to put him in the bedroom closest to the stairs. At least he wouldn't be in the room next to mine. Tough if he expected us to share a bedroom.

After I'd put new sheets on the guest room bed, I still wasn't ready to face the man downstairs, but I'd stalled enough.

Drake was just coming in from outside when I made my way back to the first floor. He was carrying a big duffel and his sniper rifle case. This was familiar. Memories of the many times he'd come home from deployment plundered my mind and heart. Usually, he left his rifle in his "cage" on base, so I wondered what location he reported to now.

I was too preoccupied reconciling my memories with my present feelings, so I didn't notice the predatory and determined look that crossed Drake's face until it was too late. He dropped his duffel and rifle to the floor, jolting me into focus.

Then he moved toward me.

No. He stalked.

He hauled me against him. I yelped.

Brawny arms wrapped around me, squeezed, until my curves were tightly pressed against the hard wall of muscles.

"I. Can. Not. Stand. It," he growled in my ear. "Three years I've dreamed of holding you in my arms." I tried to push away, but he wasn't having it. "Give me this, Iza." His breath feathered my ear, sending a shiver through my spine. "Let me hold you. Even for a few seconds. Please."

It was the *please* that did it. I relaxed slightly, stiffly.

"I love you, baby. I never stopped loving you."

"We need to talk."

Drake sighed, pulled away, and gave me his eyes. His dark, piercing eyes that seemed to skewer right into my soul. The part of me that was supposed to know him. Our faces almost touching. Our warm breaths mingling.

Excitement raced through me. The kind that was unfamiliar, dangerous, and raw. Though my heart yearned for the tenderness of the husband from my memories, the rest of my body responded at a more primal level. My brain battled with my heart to give myself permission to explore this man before me.

If it weren't for Drake's eyes, I would think I'd been sent a clone. A rougher, scarier replica of my husband.

"You look bigger." I squeezed a bicep. Drake was thickly muscled everywhere. Shoulders, chest, and back. He'd never been a slouch with fitness and always had an athletic build. Now the ridges of his muscles were more defined under his shirt. His face above his beard was leaner, cheekbones sharper.

A slash of white flashed through his face as he grinned. "Three years of celibacy. I needed an outlet."

I took a step back while heat suffused my cheeks. "Are you saying you haven't had sex—"

"Stop right there before you piss me off," Drake growled. "Unlike you, I knew I was married. I *was* married to you this whole time. I'd cut off my dick before I'd cheat on you."

I believed him. Look how long it was taking me to move on.

"And the scars?"

He fingered the area of skin on the left side of his neck. "Are you willing to listen to what happened now?"

"You won't get into trouble for it?"

Drake shrugged. "My handler knows I'm done keeping secrets from you. But I can't reveal anything about the ongoing op."

My brows furrowed. "You're not done? Are you leaving again?"

He shook his head. "No, and no. The last part of our mission will be done in-country, but I cannot tell you what it is."

I wasn't the understanding SEAL wife anymore, nor did

I want to return to that. A tendril of anger licked against my calm, reiterating to myself how circumstances had changed.

Drake eyed me warily, but there was something else. Loss. "You don't believe me."

My chin came up. "Can you blame me?"

"No." His shoulders slumped. As if years of exhaustion suddenly came crashing down on him and his next words confirmed that despite the years apart, I was still attuned to my husband's tells.

"It's been a long trip," he muttered. "Do you mind if I shower first and have coffee before we have that talk?"

I hitched my shoulders. "Not at all. I need one myself."

Our eyes locked, and heat crawled up my face.

"Separately," I added sharply.

Drake smirked. "Of course."

Drake

I SLAMMED a palm against the tiles as cum spilled all over my fist. I stroked my cock, milking my release as the spray of the shower washed over me.

When the tremors left me, I blasted the temperature of the water to freezing.

"Fuck," I grunted, struggling to let my body cool off. I'd expected Izabel's resistance. I expected a gut-punch rejection. What I didn't expect was the unleashed primitive force that refused to settle for a hug. It wanted me to throw her on the couch, possess her, and reclaim her.

And as torturous as hugging her was, it was also so fucking sweet.

Feeling her familiar curves against me. She was made for me, dammit.

I wasn't going to go all caveman and scare her away. Not upon the first meeting. I wasn't that moronic, so I quenched my thirst for her in the only way I knew how.

How I'd survived without her in the past three years. By jacking off to thoughts of her hour-glass figure. And since I'd always kept tabs on her, her image never faded.

I maneuvered my hulking frame around the tiny space of the hallway bathroom. Twenty pounds of muscle packed my frame since Izabel last saw me. I dried my back and turned to look at the burn marks and scarring. The last thing I needed from Izabel was pity, but there was no way I could hide these scars since they'd become a part of who I'd become.

Wrapping the towel around my hips, I left the bathroom. Izabel's door was closed. I planned to seduce my wife back to my bed. I could play dirty. I didn't miss the flare of desire in her eyes when our bodies were smashed together. Her body couldn't lie.

A warning blared in my head not to muddle our reconciliation with sex. I had to be smart about this and think long term.

Izabel loved me. I could feel it. Trust was the problem.

Looked like courtship wasn't out of the question.

I was looking forward to it.

. . .

I'D BEEN in the kitchen for half an hour when Izabel returned. Her long black hair was still wet from her shower, soaking part of her vee-neck white tee. She was blessed from the genetics of her mixed heritage. A heart-shaped face framed heavily lashed caramel eyes. Her luminous skin wore the shade between rich cream and light mocha. Freckles smattered her upturned nose, giving her a wicked cuteness, but her lips were crafted by alluring sin. My cock stirred as I imagined the times that mouth had wrapped around my shaft. I should have jerked off three times to take the edge off my long abstinence.

"I dumped out the coffee from this morning and brewed a new pot," I informed her as she perched on the barstool around the island.

Her brows creased adorably in both a questioning expression and a frown. I deliberately left off wearing a shirt and wore low-slung drawstring sweatpants. I rarely wore a top when I was at home because I enjoyed my wife perving playfully over my abs. On that count, she had not changed as she visibly swallowed.

"I see you're also making breakfast," Izabel said dryly. "Please make yourself at home."

"Oh, I will." I grinned as she rolled her eyes. "Coffee?"

"Yes, please."

I turned away and braced. Her gasp was instantaneous. I wanted to get the discussion of my scars out of the way.

"Drake," she whispered.

I didn't say anything, but poured her a mug of coffee,

stirred in enough milk the way she liked it, and then turned back to face her.

Tears streamed down her cheeks, but her eyes remained locked with mine.

"Don't," I muttered.

"What happened?" she asked. She tore off a sheet of paper towel and dabbed her eyes.

Waffles popped out of the toaster and stopped me from responding. I served her first, but she pushed the plate away. Maybe I was too selfish in thinking she could eat while hearing about the attack. This wasn't me and the guys shooting the shit over a campfire and trading war stories. Maybe I should have listened to the agency shrink about decompressing. I'd spent years living in another man's skin. Years not being Izabel's husband.

"Please tell me," she said softly.

"We were trapped in a cave by suicide bombers."

"Marcus said you saved him."

I clenched my jaw at her familiar use of the commander's first name. Whether it was resentment or jealousy, I wasn't sure. "It was instinctive." I shrugged. "The blast fractured my back, broke some ribs, and my right leg in three places." A ragged sob escaped her lips, but I continued, my solid gaze holding her tear-filled one. "I couldn't get back to you, Izabel, even if I wanted to. And I was helpless to protect you."

Her face crumpled, and she got off her seat, rounding the island to hug me. Izabel cried. I held tight, uncertain if she was crying out of pity or if her tears were for the losses in our marriage.

Long minutes passed before her sobs finally subsided.

Her red-rimmed eyes looked up. "I should have been there for you," she said, words garbled. "I was your wife and I couldn't help you when you needed me." She reached across the counter to grab the paper towel she used earlier to wipe her tears. Then she wiped my chest that she'd soaked. "Sorry."

"S'okay." I tenderly wiped the sorrow still streaming from her eyes with the pad of my thumb.

She sniffled a bit more and backed away, returning to her seat. "I'm ready for the rest of your story. What you can tell me, of course."

I nodded. "A task force was formed that isn't under any known government entity. I can't tell you to whom we report. However, I can tell you that it was formed out of the failure of our guys in the DoD and the CIA to perform their jobs because of our leaders in Washington."

"Isn't that treason?"

"No. It's not. We just operate differently," I said. At her continued worried frown, I added, "Trust me on this, please."

She tipped her chin. "Go on."

I explained the threat to Fire Team families. That the death of Harrelson's wife and two boys was not an accident. They were killed because our commander survived and the terrorists wanted him to suffer.

"My handler had agents on you," I said. "But their protection was contingent on me joining the task force. I had to decide quickly."

"How could they ask you to abandon your marriage just like that? And how could you agree so quickly?" Izabel snapped.

"The intel was there, baby. If I refused their offer, I'm back under DoD command. You would go unprotected. I was in no shape to organize your protection. My team and everyone I trusted was either dead, out of the country, or undercover." Even Hank was in the Middle East at that time. "I don't think the Navy ever admitted that the Commander's family was murdered."

"They said it was an accident."

"I'd rather have you hate me than see you dead."

Izabel gave a bitter smile. "And yet, that was the nightmare you gave me."

"Baby…"

She held up a hand, a rare hardness flashed in her eyes. I clamped my mouth shut.

"Did you get the terrorist?"

"Yes."

"But there's unfinished business."

"Yes."

"Am I still in danger?"

"Still assessing, but the immediate threat has been neutralized."

Izabel sipped coffee. She contemplated the brew for a beat before lifting her gaze to me. "I'm trying to be logical about this. Deep down I know you did what you thought was best for us. It was an untenable situation and quick decisions needed to be made. You say you didn't want to see me dead, but you killed me anyway. Dying isn't merely physical." She paused, rolled her lips, and her nostrils flared. "It's mental and emotional. You subjected me to that."

I gave a helpless gesture. "I know and I'm sorry."

A sad smile crossed her face and the first signs of panic coiled in my gut.

"Where do we go from here?"

Confused by her question, I narrowed my eyes. "What do you mean? I want us back together. Isn't that obvious?"

"Just like that?" The sad smile turned bitter. It was a smile I'd never witnessed on my wife's face, and I wondered now if we would ever recapture what we had.

"If there's something I'm not getting, can you spell it out?" I grated. "As soon as we nab this guy, I'll get my identity back. I know it's difficult. I've changed. You've changed, but I'm willing to put in the work to make you trust me again. I know you love me, Izabel, and I'm in love with you. That hasn't changed."

"Sometimes love isn't enough—"

"Bullshit!" I snapped. Anxiety expanded into a lump that threatened to choke me. "Why the fuck are you saying this?"

"I don't want the same things anymore," she said, voice rising. "Six years we were together, five of them as your wife. I understood and never resented each and every time you couldn't come home for Christmas or be there for our anniversary. I was happy because *you came home*. And when you were home, you were my loving husband. Sometimes I was scared out of my mind, especially when I heard the other wives talk about an op gone bad and SEALs got killed, but I held strong because when I said our vows, I committed to a life as a SEAL wife, too."

She paused and took a deep breath. "But after what happened to Fire Team and after burying a husband, I don't think I have it in me to be married to a man like you—"

"Hold on. Hold on," I cut in, trying to suppress the anger inside me. "A man like me? What the fuck, Iza?"

"A man who needs to be a hero."

"What the fuck?" I repeated. "And what man are you lookin' for now, huh, baby? Someone like your damn architect?" And this was exactly why I didn't tell her the other reason, not until I was sure she understood—if I'd abandoned the mission to hunt down Hamza, it would've eaten at me for the rest of my life and cast a shadow on our marriage. Even destroyed it.

"Maybe?" Her chin lifted mutinously.

"You're my goddamn wife!" I growled and prowled around the counter, advancing on Izabel. Her eyes widened as I plucked her from the chair. "And I'll be damned before I let another man take what's mine."

I was going to kiss her, but the fear in her eyes shocked and stopped me.

I let her go and pivoted away from her, my chest seizing in remorse. I wasn't clueless to how rough and scary I looked. I didn't need to add aggressive jealousy to it too. I exited the kitchen and dragged a hand down my face. *Chill the fuck out, asshole.*

"I didn't mean to frighten you," I said quietly.

"I'm not scared," she whispered. "Not really. It's just that…"

I turned to look at her.

"I'm not used to this new you," she said.

"Am I so different?" My hand automatically went to my beard. "I do need a beard trim."

"And a haircut," she added, biting her bottom lip. "But

there's something else. You seem harder. More rough."

The right word is savage, I thought grimly. Working under Deadly Spear, I'd lived in the skin of a hunter for three long years without a chance for respite. It was *go. Go. Go.*

I took a couple of seconds to rein in the anger that surged when she said she didn't want a "man like me" anymore. I was beginning to the see the arena I had to compete in. This wasn't going to be a simple courtship—I had to go full-court press. No way was Kyle the architect stealing my wife. It'd be a problem when she was at work. I was still operating under an assumed identity and Harrelson worked at her office.

So consumed was I in my spiraling thoughts, it took a moment to realize Izabel was speaking to me.

"Did you hear me?" she asked, frowning.

"Sorry, I was thinking about something. What was that?"

"I don't think these waffles are enough breakfast for you."

I could use a big meal right now like a bacon cheeseburger.

"The fridge is empty," she added apologetically. "I usually get my groceries on the weekends. Should we go out?"

"Any place around here that has a good breakfast?" I asked.

Izabel eyed me dubiously. "Can you be seen in public?"

"I've gotten better at sneaking around."

"Who are you? James Bond?" Izabel smiled. It was the first real smile I'd seen on her face and it was dazzling.

"Something like that." I chuckled. "I'm gonna grab a shirt. Think I want a good cheeseburger."

"I know just the place."

chapter
seven

IZABEL

I poured the rest of the coffee into my travel mug just as the microwave chimed with my leftover tostada from lunch the day before. It was Monday, two days after Drake returned to my life. After the scene in the kitchen, both of us pulled back into a cautious companionship. Tension was thick. As if we weren't sure whether we were enemies or lovers. Familiar with unfamiliar. Our dynamics had irrevocably changed. Our reality altered by the tragedy of the past three years. After lunch at the neighborhood diner, I helped Drake sort out his stuff in the attic. Our chats were on neutral topics like my job. Drake was curious about Marcus, and I told him about his problem with alcohol. Drake kept a stoic face as I updated him on his former commander's life.

Since Drake had been awake for almost forty-eight hours, he retired to his bedroom early Saturday night.

Sunday, I took him to the Glen Ford neighborhood—the site of the Solace Foundation development. Despite the uncertainty of our relationship, I felt compelled to share an important part of my current life.

The neighborhood was built in the late seventies of predominantly ranch-style homes and A-frames. When the recession of the eighties took a toll on its residents, families moved out, unable to sustain their mortgages, paving the way for the gangs to move in. The area had become a ghetto. But with the influx of immigrants in the past decade, a kind of coexistence started to take shape. The gangs were ever-present, but with the growing strength of the immigrants who were determined to make a better life for themselves, the economy in the area improved. I had gotten close to several residents. One of them was Luisa Romero, the owner of a popular taqueria in the area.

Knowing Drake had a weakness for tacos and tres leches cake made it a win-win destination, and it was a chance for me to show him my accomplishments. Although I wondered if I was uncomfortable being alone with him in the house.

Our conversations remained stilted—at least on my part. I wasn't sure what to say, what was expected of me, and how to behave. Part of me wanted to hug the man he was. My body reacted to his electric presence, but it was my mind and heart that weren't on board with simply melting into his arms.

I made a disgruntled sound as I headed over to the counter to collect the tostada. I slammed the microwave door with more strength than was necessary.

"Someone woke up on the wrong side of the bed."

I jumped and squinted at the owner of the voice. Near the entrance of the kitchen, leaning against the wall, was Drake, arms crossed and shirtless. Again. Not only that, the top button of his jeans was undone, revealing that trail of hair that sexily disappeared below the waistband. He still hadn't trimmed his beard and smirked when he caught me looking at it. He seemed more refreshed, and certainly more relaxed than I was.

Damn the man.

I knew what he was doing. Grr.

"Can you please put on a shirt when you're in the house?"

A brow shot up. "As I recall, that didn't bother you before." His lips curled into a grin. "I take that back. You loved me without my shirt on."

"Things are different now."

Something flashed in his eyes. I knew that look. It was the gleam when he wanted to throttle me but would rather fuck me instead.

Warmth tingled between my legs.

Oh, hell no.

I took a bite of my tostada. "I'm late for work," I muttered and grabbed the coffee tumbler.

"Hang on a sec. I'll take you."

I tried to dissuade him of that notion, but Drake had already disappeared up the stairs. *What the hell did he mean he'd take me?*

When my husband reappeared, casually walking up to me, I did my best to reward him with a death glare.

"You are not taking me to work."

"Yes, I am."

"Why?"

"So, I can pick you up after."

"I thought you didn't want Marcus to know you're alive just yet."

"I'm sure you'll find a way to see he doesn't find out."

I huffed in annoyance. "I have to make visits to client sites."

Drake hissed a breath. "I've got shit to do. Can't drive you around all day."

I rolled my eyes. "I wasn't expecting you to in the first place." But instead of feeling relieved that he wouldn't be chauffeuring me around, concern took over. "You got a lead on something?"

"Need to touch base with the team."

"Is that where you went last night?"

The night prior, Drake left right after dinner, saying he had some errands to run. He didn't return until two that morning. My recent insomnia kept me awake and I knew he was pacing outside my door. I held my breath for a while, thinking he'd knock, but he walked away instead.

Drake answered my question with a tight nod. No elaboration. Not a single word.

Resentment that'd been simmering over the weekend boiled over. "This isn't going to work," I burst out.

I'd surprised Drake with my reaction, judging from the flicker in his eyes.

"Give me a bit more time, baby, and I can tell—"

"Three years weren't enough?" I screamed. "Why come back now when you can't commit fully to this marriage?"

His eyes turned cold. "This isn't like you, Izabel. I have a job to do."

"I've never stopped you from doing your job." Reining in my overrun emotions, I shot him an arctic smile and yanked the door open. "So go ahead and do it."

I did my best not to slam the door. I couldn't go back to that. To barely existing. I wasn't going to waste another precious minute of my life on it. I got into my car, backed down the driveway, and motored off. When I reached the second stoplight, I noticed I was white-knuckling the steering wheel. I was gripping it tight to prevent myself from shaking. Muttering a curse, I parallel-parked beside the neighborhood sidewalk to calm myself.

I was angry.

Pissed. Off.

How did one go on after surviving the stages of grief, only to find out it was all for nothing?

WHEN I ARRIVED at the office, Cindy was already at her desk. "So," Cindy gushed as she came around to meet me. "How did it go?" The sly smile on the twenty-eight-year-old blonde confused me until I remembered my date with Kyle on Friday. That felt like ages ago after everything that happened over the weekend.

If there was one person who wanted me back in the saddle, it was Cindy. It was through her clever machinations that I ended up going to the Solace gala with Kyle, which in some way paved the way for him to ask me out.

At my pained smile, Cindy frowned. "What happened? Was he a jerk? Do I need to punch him in the nuts?"

"Slow down, slow down." I laughed at the outraged

expression on my friend's face. Clearly her loyalty was to me. "Kyle was the perfect date."

"Then what?" she squinted. "No chemistry?"

"Uh..."

"Bad kisser?"

I gave up and walked into my office.

"Bad in bed?"

"Cindy!" I exclaimed in a half-shocked, half-amused tone.

My friend chuckled. "You're so fun to mess with. Seriously though, you need to get some action."

I grimaced. "I don't think that's gonna happen anytime soon." Especially after Drake pussy-blocked me on Friday. Not that I was ready to sleep with Kyle. I was a widow—*was* being the operative word.

What a mess.

More like a disaster.

Cindy sat in the chair in front of my desk, all levity gone from her adorably freckled face. Her blue eyes searched my countenance. "Okay, Maddox. Out with it."

"I can't talk about it," I hedged.

"This isn't about Drake, is it?" Cindy's voice was so gentle, it made me cringe. "He's been gone for three years. He would want you to find happiness again."

I burst into hysterical laughter, startling my friend, but I couldn't stop even when it sounded more like a cackle of bitterness than amusement. And once the laughter started, I couldn't stop. Tears burned my eyes. I couldn't determine if I wanted to laugh or cry.

Cindy grew alarmed. "Izabel, if you don't say anything—"

I pressed a forearm across my stomach because the spontaneous laughter started to hurt somewhere in the vicinity of my diaphragm. I held up a finger to signal Cindy to give me a moment.

"I'm sorry." I gulped a deep breath and tried not to think that my "dead" husband wasn't really dead. "I'd love to talk about it, but not right now."

Cindy crossed her arms over her chest. "Something happened between Friday and now. I wish I had checked on you over the weekend, but I didn't want to interrupt…just in case." She resumed her teasing and waggled her brows.

A short laugh that was completely genuine this time escaped my lips. "Okay, Lake, we've got a busy day ahead."

Cindy rose from the chair and clucked her tongue. "You've got a busy day with site visits. I'm stuck in the office all day while you get to spend time with hunky Harrelson. Hey, do you think he and I…?"

I cleared my throat as I looked over Cindy's shoulder at the tall, sandy-haired gentleman who appeared at the door.

Cindy froze, face paling. "He's standing behind me, isn't he?"

"I didn't hear anything," Marcus drawled. Drake's former commander still had an imposing look about him, but tragedy had taken its toll, evident in the brackets around his mouth and a smile that didn't reach his eyes.

And now it was hard to meet his gaze, much less imagining spending an entire day with him.

Flustered, I shuffled papers on my desk. "I don't think I need your escort today, Marcus."

The dead silence in the room forced me to look up. I

ignored Cindy's penetrating stare and held Marcus's flinty regard.

"Something going on, Izzy?" Marcus asked, tone level.

I shrugged. "No. Why do you say that?" My tone went high-pitched with those last two words, so much so that I couldn't help wincing.

"She's been acting strangely this morning," Cindy announced, crossing her arms again.

"Uh-huh, I can see that." Marcus mimicked her movement.

"I'm right here, people," I muttered, dropping onto my chair and spinning around to give them my back as I woke up my laptop to go through emails. "The Solace Foundation site visit in Glen Ford is in the middle of the afternoon, and I've made enough friends in the community to be comfortable among them."

Marcus grunted his displeasure. "I gave you my report on them last week."

"And I appreciate it, but I can't be walking around their neighborhood with an armed escort beside me."

"Tell me the reason again?" Marcus challenged. "Because we've played it so I'm your driver and not your bodyguard. So why is it suddenly a problem?"

I swiveled around and faced him. "I can't be a hypocrite. I fought so hard for this project. We gained enough sponsors because I believed in the industriousness of the immigrant population. Given the same chance and the same support as everyone else, they can realize their American dreams. If I show up with a bodyguard every time, it's like I don't trust them to live a life other than being a criminal."

His face softened. "I get you now, but as part of this company's security team, let me be the judge. All right?"

I was about to protest when Marcus held up his hand. "Can't mess up, Izzy. I'm on probation right now and the evaluation of the Solace site is ongoing. We can't let idealism trump operational procedure, especially after Bose got attacked by one of his foremen."

Well, Mr. Bose could be an asshole, as I remembered the lone dissenter in the boardroom when I proposed the Solace project. It was a good thing the other owner, Mr. Stockman, threw his support behind me.

"Whew, so that's settled, right?" Cindy asked. "Marcus's going with you?"

I sighed. "Guess so."

My driver/bodyguard glanced at his phone. "We've got Little Creek at ten, Newport News at one, and Glen Ford at three. Sound good?"

"Sounds about right." I leaned back against my chair. "Thanks, Marcus."

He tipped his chin at us, pivoted on his heel, and strode out the door.

Cindy bit her bottom lip. "Now that's a gorgeous ass."

"Stop drooling."

"Hey, I know he's not interested, okay? I just want to take care of him."

"He's a forty-four-year-old man. And how old are you?"

She scowled at me. "You know what I mean, and don't tell me you were never worried about him."

"He's been sober for six months. I'm very hopeful this time." Cindy was more concerned for Marcus as a friend, just as most in the company were rallying around him. It sucked to be the poster boy for a tragic past, and I wished Marcus was blessed with anonymity. But his story was too big, and an overzealous reporter exposed Drake's commander, compromising his identity as a SEAL. But Marcus was too broken to even be considered for active duty. He hadn't eaten his gun. He'd battled his demons. Apprehension rose inside me. How would Marcus react once he found out Drake was alive and confirmed that terrorists murdered his family?

A knock on the open door drew our eyes. Kyle stood there looking clean-cut and handsome in his expensive suit. The company brought him on as a senior manager for our commercial development department and had all the interns swooning at his feet with his golden-boy good looks.

The little spark that I'd felt for him last Friday had fizzled with the return of the dangerously sexy version of my husband. A stubborn part of me was mad at myself, but a larger part of me was relieved.

"Am I interrupting something?" Kyle asked uncertainly. Concern drew his brows together.

Cindy winced. "Uh, I'm out of here."

I shot her a some-friend-you-are look. I hadn't prepared my breakup speech. *Wait*, was there even something to break up? We'd been on one date.

As if reading my mind, Kyle's shoulders drooped and disappointment washed over his features. "You're backing out on our date Wednesday."

"Something's come up."

Kyle gave a tight nod. "Tell me honestly. Did I come on too strong?"

"Friday night was perfect," I said huskily. "I can't explain right now, but it's nothing you did."

He was quiet for a while, looking at a spot on the carpet, as if contemplating his words carefully, then he raised his gaze. "Did I imagine our connection at dinner?"

I gave a slight shake of my head. "No, you didn't."

Another tight nod, followed by a long exhale. "I think I know why, but I'm not going to push you on it. You'll have to open up your heart in your own time, Izabel. I'm willing to wait."

He walked to the door, but paused right by the frame, turning back to me. "Your husband would want you to be happy. Think of that. In the meantime, I can be patient." He smiled, his face brightening with determination. "You're worth it."

When he left, I buried my face in my hands. Aggravation stretched my already high-strung nerves.

The universe must be laughing.

chapter
eight

DRAKE

I PARKED the Escalade along the sidewalk of a small stretch of commercial buildings. Exiting the vehicle, I walked up to a nondescript gray building a few blocks from where I'd parked. From the outside, it looked abandoned and a big sign on several entrances stated that the building was condemned by the city.

It was a front, because I'd been here the night before. A rust-colored iron door sealed the back exit, and a metal mailbox was mounted on the wall at around chest level. The contraption was not used for mail.

I inserted a security card through the fake slot. Rotors whirred, and a shield slid down to expose a one-inch by six-inch display with a keypad beneath it. I entered a nine-digit code and bent down for a retinal scan. The shield slid closed, followed by gears and tumblers moving. The tight seal slackened and spit out my security card. The mechanism would have destroyed the access card if the retinal scan and code hadn't matched up.

I pushed down on a lever and pulled open the door. Motion sensors triggered the lights, illuminating a drab hallway. The ancient interior was spotless. Vinyl tiles covered the floors and fluorescent fixtures hanging from equally clinical ceiling tiles gave the illusion of an underground operation. Camera spheres mounted at every corner recorded my arrival.

My footsteps were conspicuous echoes in the hallway's silence. I turned and entered the last room. A collapsible table and several folding chairs littered an otherwise empty space. A huge cabinet sat near the wall. Except it wasn't a cabinet. Hidden buttons along a side panel activated rollers to move the fixture enough for a man of my size to move into a space in the wall and enter the car of a hidden elevator.

With the scissor gates closed, the lights along the edges of the interior activated. Flipping open an access panel, I entered a code and the floor below me moved as the elevator descended below ground.

The basement had been a bomb shelter in the sixties. Unlike the rest of the building, it was completely renovated and tricked out with the latest technology, including a holographic map and glass projector screen at the center of the room. A stack of servers hummed in the corner with a direct link to the CIA, NSA, and other federal databases. Wi-Fi connection was highly encrypted.

Castle Rock—our task force's base.

Our analyst, Tim, was in one corner, processing data.

Edmunds and Brick were sitting around a conference table. Viktor stood at the head of the table, poring over some documents and, without looking at me, said, "Glad you could join us, Maddox."

Fuck you, Viktor. I didn't regret my tardiness. I'd discovered something in Izabel's office at home that had gutted me. The temptation to blow off this meeting and confront Izabel at once was strong, but I reminded myself that the sooner we closed the loop on the task force's mission, the sooner I could return to my life with her. My chest spasmed at the idea that I could be too late, that my wife had truly moved on.

Or she didn't want to go back to being my wife.

I nodded at the other two men in the room, who returned my greeting with chin lifts. The grin on Brick's face told me he was enjoying whatever anti-bromance I was having with Viktor. Finally, the man in question glanced up, studying my face. The slight narrowing of his ice-blue eyes felt like a blade scraping layers off my skin.

"You okay, Maddox?"

Why deny this shit was okay? "Feeling a bit raw."

"Something happen with Izabel?"

I clenched my jaw and shook my head, hating the drilling stare from the other man. "No. Can we get this meeting started? Got shit to do."

"Oh, definitely..." Viktor replied. He looked at Edmunds and Brick. "Give us five minutes."

A look of surprise came from the other two men when Viktor headed to the back room, tipping his chin at me to follow him. Blowing out a breath, I trudged after him. Whatever Viktor had to say couldn't bring me down any lower. Maybe he'd kick me off the team, although the look on his face was far from irritated. I would even say it was almost…pitying.

Which was worse.

When we reached the far corner, Viktor faced me. He was an inch taller than my six-three, so we were more or less eye-to-eye.

"Kept you guys waiting…sorry." I grimaced. "I needed time to sort myself out."

"Can you do your job?"

"What exactly is my job?" I derided. "What the hell am I working for if I've lost everything I want to live for?"

"Groveling not working, I take it?"

"Fuck you," I growled. "Cut this shit and get to the point."

"We will, but we need to sort out your ass."

"Got a headshrinker for that."

"Maybe Izabel needs to see Carter, too?"

Dr. Gina Carter was a good friend of Viktor's and a retired agency shrink. Somehow, he had convinced the doctor to fly over to Germany during my recovery from back surgery. Viktor didn't believe in wasting time and wanted me to work on my mental, as well as physical, recovery. Basically, ensuring I didn't break down and return to Izabel before the mission was complete.

"What? Like couple's counseling?"

"You make it sound like a bad thing."

"Doc G would do that?"

"She's retired," Viktor said dryly. "Gina has nothing else to do but play golf."

"Izabel's having second thoughts about staying married to me." Bile rose up my throat as I looked away from the older man and brushed the cold sweat from my upper lip.

"Give her time to adjust to you."

"How long?" I fidgeted in place. Thinking about staying away from Izabel was making it hard to keep the panic from crawling out of my skin.

"Jesus, Maddox, I don't fucking know."

"Not giving her space." Especially with that damn architect sniffing at her heels.

"Somehow, I'm not surprised," the other man drawled. "Underneath your perceived betrayal, she'll realize that you made the best and most logical decision for the both of you."

I emitted a bitter laugh. "She's also come to her senses that I'm a bad bet."

"Stop whining."

"Fuck you."

A few seconds of testosterone-charged air hung between us. Until Viktor's brow shot up. "You good?"

"Yeah…" Surprisingly, using him as a sounding board to release my frustration was very helpful.

"Good. Because I ain't talking about feelings." Viktor moved past me to walk back to the conference table.

"You started it," I muttered.

A brief chuckle escaped Viktor's lips. "Just wanted you to know that Carter is available to you."

"Thanks."

"No problem."

Out of our task force, only Edmunds and Brick returned to the East Coast. The rest of the men disbanded to retire or pursue other things. Though most of our team were handpicked because of skill set, each one had a personal stake whether to avenge our fallen brothers or to end Youssef Hamza. At this stage, we were more dependent on spy craft to determine the leak of operational information that compromised the JSOC mission. Their deaths had scored my soul and bringing all the people responsible to justice was the only way the scar wouldn't blister and bleed.

Viktor grabbed the glass display controller and clicked several times to show a list of numbers and several overlapping circles, which I interpreted as cell phone triangulation.

"We recovered a list of cell phone numbers from Hamza's files," Viktor said. "Most of them are burners and scattered around Africa, Europe, and the Middle East, but we've shut down most of those cells over the past three years." He clicked and changed the screen to what looked like a map of the eastern seaboard centering on Virginia. "With the list of numbers from Hamza's files, we were able to isolate these cell phone clouds. Tim's algorithm along with archived data from the NSA plotted two clouds over DC and Virginia Beach at around the timeframe of the joint Fire Team and Delta Force mission."

"Are you saying we had a blatant breach of operational security?" Brick asked incredulously.

"Yes," Viktor clipped, magnifying the cell phone clouds. "The one over DC was active two hours before that mission. Someone was feeding Hamza real-time information."

Curses erupted between Brick and Edmunds, but my attention zeroed in on a particular spot on the display.

"That date over the VA Beach cloud…that was four days before we shipped out," I speculated.

Viktor nodded grimly. "Multiple transmissions between Hamza and that number have been confirmed on the days leading to your team's deployment and we've identified who was at the location."

The look on the task force chief twisted a knot of apprehension in my gut. "You have a name?"

It was more a statement than a question.

Again, Viktor nodded. "Guardians are keeping an eye on him, but we received a ninety-nine percent confirmation from Tim's app this morning."

"Do we know where he is?"

"We're ready to bring him in."

"Great!" I sprang from the chair, a devil of a purpose driving my actions. "Let's smoke the motherfucker."

"You're sitting this one out."

"What the fuck, Baran?" I growled, but the other man's expression sent my thoughts into a wild trajectory, a path my brain did its best to reject, but the truth was written all over Viktor's face.

Slowly, I approached the area where Viktor stood, and picked up the display controller from the table and clicked. Anger and betrayal burned a hole in my chest.

"Son of a bitch!"

chapter
nine

Izabel

It was almost three in the afternoon when the company vehicle pulled in front of the ruins of several dilapidated houses in the Glen Ford neighborhood.

"Stick close to me," Marcus said when I was about to open my side of the door.

He got out of the vehicle and immediately turned his attention to our surroundings. Tractors, bulldozers, and demolition crews were already on site to clear the area where new single-family homes and an apartment building were going to be erected. The Metro Bank and the Solace Foundation partnered on the project financing. Stockman and Bose had offered their services—manpower and materials at a discounted rate—including the architectural design work for free. My team was spearheading this project.

"I don't see King," Marcus said as he slipped on his aviators.

I checked my phone and noted a missed message from him. "He's going to be thirty minutes late. Traffic on Sixty-Four."

"Izabel!"

Luisa, the taqueria owner, was fast approaching with excitement in her eyes. "So it's really happening?"

Her glee was infectious and exactly what I needed on this confusing day. "Yes. It's happening."

She clutched her chest. "God bless you, child. From now on, you and your man will have tacos for life."

Luisa meant Drake, but it was Marcus who gave a pained cough, thinking she was referring to him. Heart in throat, I laughed nervously.

"About operating a taco truck in front of your building," the woman continued. "I appreciate the offer, but with my son off to college, we will be shorthanded. I'm sure me and my familia will be slinging more tacos than we can handle with construction starting."

"That's true," I agreed. We discussed the influx of business to the area brought about by the development. After a few minutes, Luisa bade goodbye and walked back to her taqueria.

"It just occurred to me," Marcus started casually. "That Mrs. Romero wasn't referring to me."

"She wasn't." I put on sunglasses before I nimbly hopped around the debris on the sidewalk.

"Are you seeing someone, Izzy?"

I was saved from answering when a bulldozer dumped

debris into a pile, drowning out every other noise in our surroundings. Instead, I made a circling motion with my forefinger, signaling to *look around*. I was anxious to see the spot where we were building the children's playground, with the added intent for Marcus to drop the question.

He came up behind me as I headed down the length of the deserted stretch of houses and was reminded of Marcus's concerns. Although most of the current residents gladly moved out of their homes, there were some who were resistant. Metro Bank bought up their existing mortgages and gave them a stipend to rent an apartment while the eighteen-month development was ongoing. It was more than a fair deal, given what they would have spent to keep their houses livable. But, as with all negotiations, there were some who weren't happy moving elsewhere—especially those who used the houses for drug deals.

After working on exclusive subdivisions with perfectly manicured landscaping and state-of-the-art clubhouses, I wanted a development that would give the residents a sense of home. One where the children could play, get dirty, scrape their knees, and run around with the family dog.

Economic growth was imminent in the Newport News area and I wanted the Glen Ford residents to be a part of it. Most of the community came from Latinx or Asian backgrounds. My own mother was a second-generation Colombian immigrant who, upon graduating from high school, worked two jobs so she could afford to go to beauty school. I understood the value of hard work, the fear of losing a roof over my head, and going to bed hungry.

I was forever grateful to Mr. Stockman for giving me this

opportunity to fulfill a childhood idealistic dream, which brought my ambivalence about Drake's return into focus. Would I have been so driven in the pursuit of this project if Drake hadn't "died"? The hours I put into chasing down every sponsor to donate to the Solace Foundation had been my coping mechanism for losing my husband and baby.

His return made me feel like a fraud. Like I just used this project as my therapy instead of genuinely caring for Luisa and the residents.

"Goddammit." Marcus's muttered curse yanked me out of my musings.

"What…?" My question cut off with the approach of two dangerous-looking men. I'd never seen them before, and they certainly didn't look like they belonged in Glen Ford.

"Don't look at them." Marcus moved closer. The demolition activity was some distance behind us. The noise it was producing would drown out any calls of help. "Keep walking."

Heart pounding, I did as I was told, but luck wasn't with us. We were definitely on the newcomers' radar.

Marcus slipped in front of me just as the strangers stopped before us.

"Whassup," Marcus said.

The ginger-haired man's smile was shark-like. "We need both of you to come with us. Quietly." Though the man was dressed like a homie, his military bearing gave him away.

Marcus puffed a derisive laugh. "No can do, bro." He cupped my bicep and backed us away. "Whoever hired you guys to intimidate the developers can go fuck themselves."

Ginger-Hair lowered his gaze to Marcus's side where I

figured he had his hand on his gun. Ginger-Hair's companion grew alert and moved his hand, likely to reach for his firearm.

Shit.

"There's no need for that, Marcus," Ginger-Hair said softly.

My friend froze.

"Who the fuck are you guys?" Marcus growled.

Ginger-Hair shrugged. "If you come with us, we can tell you. I can't believe you'd put Drake's wife in danger."

Indignation dissolved my fear and fueled my bravado. "Tell my husband he can go fuck himself. Marcus and I have a job to do."

I spun around and marched off, expecting the men to respect my wishes. I couldn't believe this was how Drake intended to tell Marcus he was alive! Scaring us like this. What if Marcus reacted and someone got shot?

A scuffle erupted behind me, and I turned in time to see Marcus taken down by Ginger-Hair and his cohort.

"What are you guys doing?" I shrieked.

A hand clamped over my mouth, and I was yanked against a hard chest.

Marcus's eyes widened at the man behind me before Ginger-Hair stuck a needle in his neck.

"Sorry it has to be this way, Iza," Drake's voice murmured in my ear before he half-lifted, half-dragged me in between two houses and bundled me into a waiting van. Drake got in beside me. Ginger-Hair and his partner carried Marcus. A few of Glen Ford residents watched the scene unfold, but just like they were taught to do to survive in the rough neighborhood, they turned away.

Marcus was dumped in the back of the van, and his head hit the side of the vehicle.

"Be careful!" I yelled, then spun on Drake. "Why are you doing this? Why are you treating Marcus like this? Hasn't he been through enough?"

Drake's eyes were cold. "He has a lot to answer for."

"What are you talking about?"

"Can't tell you yet."

A derisive huff escaped my lips. "Figures."

"But I will."

"When? Will that be your story after another three years of pretending you're dead?"

The van pulled away from the curb and sped off to the back streets away from the development.

"Enough!" Drake growled. "If you can't forgive me for what I've done, there's nothing else I can do."

A feeling akin to fear and panic gripped my heart. "What do you mean?"

Drake sighed. "If you can't trust me again, then maybe it's best if we stay separated for a while instead of tearing each other apart like this."

Oh! He was giving up? Didn't I have the right to come to terms with the fact that I'd been lied to and made to suffer for three years? Tears burned the back of my eyes. A stricken look replaced the anger on Drake's face. "Iza…"

"Maybe it's for the best." My chin tipped up, feeling stubborn, holding on to my indignation, my fury. *How dare he*? "Better yet, don't change your name back to Drake Maddox and we won't have to separate or divorce or anything. Let the dead stay buried."

I couldn't stand the sight of him and looked out the window. The awkward silence in the van made me aware that in my anger, I'd forgotten we had an audience. Drake remained quiet beside me except for the rustle of his clothes as he moved.

My phone vibrated with a text from Mr. King. I gripped my phone, undecided on how to reply, and my sheer inability to do so only frayed my high-strung nerves.

I'd been building a life without him, but Drake and his secrets were ruining it.

———

Drake

Izabel fumed beside me.

I was pissed at myself for losing patience with my wife, but Marcus's betrayal hit me hard. And now words were spoken between us that could never be unsaid.

Let the dead stay buried.

Five words. Five words that hollowed my chest and shredded my heart. Maybe Viktor was right, and we needed a mediator because I sure as hell was digging myself into a deeper hole. I knew fuck all how to reach her.

"I had a very important meeting with the foundation manager," Izabel spoke tightly. She was not looking at me, but out the window. "You and your friends better have a good excuse to give my office."

"We'll have Tim leave an anonymous tip that you and

Harrelson were abducted," Brick said. "Your company vehicle is still at the site. I'm Brick, by the way." He thumbed at our driver. "He's Edmunds."

Izabel was shaking her head. "This was Marcus's last chance to prove himself." Sadness tinged her voice. I wanted to grab her and roar that he was a traitor who never deserved to live. "You've ruined that for him, too. Has he not suffered enough?"

Not even close.

"There's a good reason we took Harrelson," Brick said.

"More than a few saw you guys haul us away."

"We're taking care of that," Edmunds piped in for the first time.

"What does that mean?" Izabel asked incredulously.

Viktor had someone pay them off. But no one was volunteering to enlighten her.

Izabel's phone kept on pinging with text messages.

"Better turn that off, sweet cheeks," Brick said.

"Don't call her that," I growled.

He chuckled. "Sorry, chief."

"Where are you taking us?" she asked as our vehicle entered the interstate.

Edmunds' eyes met mine in the rearview mirror.

"Got it," I muttered, hating to have to do this part because it was gonna be another reason for her to hate me.

Izabel turned away from the scenery. Wariness stole over her face as her eyes pinged between me and the guys. One thing was certain; she still could sense my change in tone when something was wrong. "Got what?"

"I have to do this, baby." Her beautiful eyes widened in surprise before I threw the hood over her.

chapter ten

DRAKE

I CARRIED my unconscious wife into Castle Rock's basement. Hooding Izabel had been the last straw for her; I didn't recognize the screeching banshee that cursed me behind the black fabric. Not only that, she'd become violent, attacked me with her nails that I was left with no choice except to sedate her.

This was what my betrayal had done to our marriage.

Izabel possessed her mother's fiery temper, but she'd never physically hurt me. Although I'd seen her rant on more than one occasion, both of us treasured our time together, and we kept our drama to a minimum. I found her annoyed outbursts at me cute, which infuriated her more. That was when I'd woo with sweetness.

This was not the same.

This was anger and grief and deep-rooted trauma all rolled into one.

I'd noticed the changes in her. A hardness about her and I couldn't decide whether it was a good or a bad thing.

She'd become this way because of me.

Tim glanced up from his computer and winced. "We've got a cot behind those dividers."

"Thanks." I prowled to the area where the analyst had pointed.

"Where's Harrelson?"

"They're prepping him upstairs for interrogation." I lowered Izabel carefully to the bed, making sure she was in a comfortable position. I crouched beside her, already having removed the hood, and took in her peaceful face. Between us, I was the early riser and my favorite morning activity besides sex was watching her sleep. My hand reached out to stroke her forehead. "I'm sorry, Iza."

I stayed with her for a few more minutes until the unwelcome buzz of my phone let me know they needed me in the interrogation room. I hated leaving Izabel in a strange place, but she was secure here. Her trust in our marriage had evaporated, but I hope she still trusted me to keep her safe.

"I'll keep an eye on her," Tim offered.

I glanced at the bespectacled analyst who looked more like Clark Kent than the typical SF operator. It was probably best my wife didn't wake up to one of my rough-looking teammates. Three years chasing terrorists across the Middle East, Europe, and Africa had left an indelible mark on all our faces. It wasn't just the beard or the unkempt hair; it was an overall stamp—almost visceral, yet the sharp edges were there...a feral glint in a hunter's eye.

"Thanks." Rising from my crouch, I headed to the elevator and took the car to the first floor. I exited the elevator room and crossed the hallway to the room diagonally across from it. It was the only other area in the building that Viktor had extensively renovated. I entered the darkened space, lit by a lone light bulb strung out from the ceiling. The windowless room was reinforced with soundproofed gray walls.

At that moment, Marcus Harrelson sat in a chair in front of a simple desk. His wet hair indicated he had a rude awakening. Brick stood in front of him while Edmunds was busy prepping the sensory dissonance equipment. A tall form stood in the shadows.

Marcus's eyes tracked my arrival.

"Drake...? You're alive?" he asked hoarsely. "Where's Izabel?"

Fury scalded my insides. "Don't ever mention her name, you motherfucker."

His eyes flashed, equally furious. "Is this a game, Lieutenant? Why are you here? You're fucking dead. Explain to me what the fuck is going on."

I exchanged a glance with Brick, signaling that I was taking over the interrogation.

"I survived the massacre, but Izabel was in danger and I couldn't return."

"Dianne...the kids..." Marcus's face crumpled. "It was because of Fire Team, wasn't it? It wasn't an accident."

Though I believed Marcus wouldn't put his family in jeopardy, it didn't excuse his betrayal. "You should have known better than to make deals with terrorists!"

Harrelson struggled in his chair. "Would someone tell me what the fuck is going on?"

"Days before Fire Team shipped out, where were you?"

"I…I was in a hotel."

"Dianne kicked you out."

"We'd been separated for months," Marcus gritted. "What does that have to do with anything?"

"There were calls between Hamza and a number in Virginia Beach. Cell cloud algorithms showed an intersection over the Marquis Hotel."

"What—Are you saying I betrayed my own men?"

"How do you explain the cell phone records?"

"That proves nothing."

"Doesn't it?" I growled. "Tell me, Harrelson, what did Hamza offer you?"

"I'm telling you, Maddox! Your intel is wrong. What would I gain? I've washed out of rehab twice. Losing Fire Team, my family…does any of this make sense?"

"Guilt, Harrelson. Guilt that your treachery killed your wife and kids."

"And yet, I would have died if you didn't shield me."

That was what bugged me about the entire thing. Marcus would have died, too.

"Get me out of these restraints." Spittle flew and Marcus's face mottled with fury as he shook in his chair again.

"The VP's chief of staff. How well do you know her?" Viktor asked as he walked out from the shadows.

"Allison?"

"Allison Tierney," Viktor said silkily. "Rumor has it Vice President Colbert is being groomed to run for president."

"What does Ally have to do with anything?"

"She had operational knowledge of the mission."

"She was present at the briefings, yes."

"Do you know that some of Colbert's biggest supporters are the oil companies operating in Africa?"

"Same for every other fucking politician." Marcus squinted his eyes. "I know who you are, Baran. What you do. I heard rumors of a shadow force operating unplugged from the DoD and CIA. That's you guys. Am I right?"

I stepped back, giving Viktor the floor. Apparently, there was a political angle none of the team was aware of.

"You mentioned Youssef Hamza," Harrelson stated as the name of the terrorist registered. "Wasn't he…?" He turned to me. "Sudan?"

"Yes."

"This is about Sudan," Marcus swallowed hard.

"He became the puppet master behind every modern terrorist network."

Harrelson bowed his head, giving it a shake before he glanced back at me. "I gave the order that killed his family." His lids slid shut and tears escaped the corners of his eyes. "Dianne, Adam, and Joe—they're really dead because of me." His shoulders shook as he was wracked with sobs.

Viktor and I exchanged glances.

What's next?

Viktor gave Harrelson a few minutes to collect himself before he spread the photos on the table.

"These are pictures of Tierney and the CEO of Exetron Oil," Viktor said. "Terrorist groups in Africa have been giving the company problems."

Ignoring the photos on the table, Marcus glared at me. "Tell me Hamza is dead."

I nodded, and it was only then that Marcus gave his attention to the photographs. "Ally mentioned their problems with the terrorists in passing." He sniffed as a shudder rippled through him. The revelation had shocked his system and his lips were bloodless.

I leaned in closer as I picked up how my former commander used Tierney's name with familiarity.

Apparently, so did Viktor. "What exactly is your relationship to Tierney?"

"When Dianne and I..." His shoulders pulled back as if in realization. "Jesus Christ, I'm such a fucking idiot. Ally and I had a brief affair..."

Viktor went in for the kill. "You had an affair with Tierney while you were separated from your wife? Can you give us a timeline?"

"Three months, on and off, but we were together the week up until we deployed."

"Did she stay with you at the hotel?"

"Yeah..."

"Did she have access to your phone?"

"I'm so stupid," Marcus muttered. "I never thought Ally..."

"Could the signal be coming from Tierney's burner and not Marcus's?" I asked. This could certainly be a game changer. Marcus didn't have a motive; Tierney did.

"Possibly," Viktor said. "The numbers are different, but she could have used different burners."

"So, she already had operational information because of her position as Chief of Staff," Brick interjected. "And she's the one feeding information to Hamza? But why even bother with Marcus?"

"The Teams," Marcus gave me a tortured expression. "She was very interested in our personal stuff. Family life. I'm an idiot," he repeated. "She played me...I thought she was sympathetic to our lives...the challenge of getting deployed and coming home. Something Dianne had grown to resent and what tore our marriage apart. Jesus...she played me."

"Hamza had a very detailed file on every single member of Fire Team," Viktor said. "Granted, Tierney has access to every SEAL's file, but this is personal to Hamza. He wanted to hit the SEALs where it hurt."

"I'm gonna kill her," Marcus whispered fiercely, eyes flaring. "I'm gonna kill that fucking bitch." He shook his restraints again. "Let me go!"

"Not so fast," Viktor said. "I'm not quite convinced you had no part in this."

"Are you insane?" Marcus roared. "Get me out of this fucking chair."

I had a surge of sympathy for Marcus, and the way his life was so fucked up spoke for itself, but there was still not enough evidence to eliminate him completely as a suspect.

"Maddox," Viktor said. "Outside."

I was ready for a break. Already raw from my situation with Izabel, it gutted me I'd misread Harrelson's situation. We were brothers. I should have trusted him. These past three years had changed me in a fundamental way. The concept of brotherhood had been erased since we'd operated sometimes on our own.

Marcus continued to lose his shit while we exited the room. After the door closed, Viktor crossed his arms and braced his legs.

"What do you think?"

I emitted a brief, derisive chuckle. "You're asking me?"

"Do you trust Harrelson?"

"I did. Then I didn't. Now? I'm not sure anymore."

"Gut?"

I exhaled a heavy breath rife with uncertainty. "I knew he was having problems with Dianne, but I didn't expect he would have an affair."

"He was separated."

I was being unfair. But if Izabel asked me for a separation, the last thing I'd do would be to jump in bed with another woman. I'd panic and pull everything from my arsenal to win her back, to find out where I'd failed and fix what was broken.

"Not everyone has what you have with Izabel, Maddox," Viktor said. His uncanny ability to read the room was unnerving. "Don't let that cloud your judgment on the matter at hand."

"I trusted him with my life."

"Would you trust him with your life now?"

"No."

Reclaiming Izabel

A blond brow shot up.

"Marcus isn't in a good place. He just found out I'm alive. He's only six months out of rehab and has got murder on his mind." Not that I blamed the man. "Using him as an asset now is risky."

"But?"

"It could also be an advantage. He's got motivation." And there was a fire in Marcus's eyes the last time he demanded to be freed.

My phone buzzed with a text from Tim. Izabel was awake.

"I need to get back." I had my own problems to deal with. "I'm the last person to make a decision about Marcus."

"Agreed." Viktor nodded toward the elevator room. "Go to Izabel. Spend time with her. Did you inject her with the BloodTrak serum?"

BloodTrak was a tracker created with nanotechnology that bound to the host's blood cells and was untraceable by most tracker wands.

"Yes."

"Good. Take her to see Carter or get her out of town."

"How about her job? The police have to be looking for them."

"We'll handle it. For now, we're putting the blame on the local chapter of Fuego." Fuego was the notorious gang with ties to the Mexican cartel and had been known for violent executions.

"Will her abduction jeopardize the project? It might spook the bank and the foundation sponsoring the development."

Viktor's mouth turned up at one corner. "I think we've

given the cops a reason to tighten the leash on the gang's activities. I'd say we've done the development a favor."

I chuckled despite my apprehension that Izabel wouldn't see it the same way. "Better see how my wife is doing."

"Good luck."

chapter
eleven

DRAKE

"Izabel?"

I approached her carefully. She was huddled at the edge of the cot, knees drawn to her chest with her arms around them. I glanced back at Tim and mouthed, *What happened?*

The analyst hitched his shoulders; worry creased his forehead.

"Iza?"

"I have a headache," she whispered, voice scratchy.

A glass of water and Advil sat on the small table beside the cot. Obviously, she didn't trust anyone enough to take it.

"You hooded me." Brown eyes glared at me.

"Iza—"

"You tranq'd me."

I had no defense because I did those things.

"You've changed." She lowered her eyes to the floor, lips

quivering. "The Drake I knew would never do those things. He wouldn't do anything that would hurt me." She rubbed her forehead.

"And I never would," I gritted. "You were going to hurt yourself fighting me."

"Why didn't you blindfold me instead?"

I glanced back at Tim, who'd moved to the far end of the room to give us privacy. I stepped closer to Izabel.

"Because that's our thing," I said, voice low. "I didn't want to taint our memories of something beautiful."

Her lips twisted into a sneer that made me bristle. "So you decided it was better to scare me than to ruin our silly sex games?"

Silly? I could be an ass and remind her how much she enjoyed being blindfolded, naked, with her hands gripping the brass frame of the bed while I spread her legs and devoured her pussy.

Dammit. I probably shouldn't have thought of that memory either. Craving her taste was becoming unbearable.

"I didn't think you'd react that way. I was with you, Iza. You knew I would never let anything hurt you."

"Don't you get it? You're not the man I remember. How many times do I need to tell you? You're a stranger."

"Then it's time to get to know your husband again." I tried to caress her face, but she jerked away from my touch. I ground my molars, beating back the bitterness and defeat that was threatening to bury me. I nodded to the water and Advil. "Take that and let's go."

"Where's Marcus?" It was as if a cloud lifted from her

brain and she grew alert. "What have you done to him? Why did you hurt him?"

"He's a SEAL. What we did to him was nothing." At least, nothing compared to Marcus finding out his part in his family's death.

"You might have gotten him fired."

"Good!" I stalked out from the confines of the divider. She didn't immediately follow me, but the slamming of the water glass indicated she'd taken the Advil. Her footsteps echoed behind me before she condemned me with her gaze once more.

"How can you say that? He's your friend."

"After this, I'm not so sure. And I mean, it would be good if he was fired because he could do better things."

Her eyes widened. "You're recruiting him? Was kidnapping us some kind of test?" Her eyes wandered around our command center, pursing her lips before returning her eyes to mine, waiting for an answer.

"That's not how it works." I stepped into the elevator and she hurried in beside me.

"My purse?"

"In my car."

The sounds of the elevator echoed loudly in our silence. I pulled the scissor gates open just as Marcus, flanked by Viktor and Brick, emerged.

"Marcus!" Izabel cried as she ran toward our friend before I could stop her.

Jealousy stabbed my chest followed by the unexpected fury locking my muscles because if I could've moved, I would have yanked her back against me. Viktor recognized the volatility of the situation and inserted himself between Izabel and Harrelson, stopping my wife from reaching Marcus.

"Who the hell are you?" Izabel screeched.

"Your husband's boss."

"He's not my husband."

Viktor smirked. "I agree."

Glaring at Viktor over the top of Izabel's head, I gripped her shoulders and flattened her back against me.

"Are you okay?" She tried to look past the mountain that was Viktor.

"I'm fine, Izzy. Go with Drake."

"But—"

"Come on. Let's go." My hands slid to her upper arms and led her toward the back exit.

"Drake," Viktor called.

He pointed two fingers to his eyes.

"Fuck," I muttered.

Brick approached us and handed me a hood.

Mutiny was written all over Izabel's face as her eyes dared me to put the covering over her.

"I have no choice."

"I'm not stopping you."

I was beginning to hate those four words with a passion.

And with her eyes cutting right through the heart of me, I put the offending layer over her head and prepared for a hellish night.

"This isn't the way home," Izabel said.

"I'm not taking you to your house."

"What's going on?"

I removed the hood the second we got on the interstate. Izabel didn't freak out or argue this time. I wondered if I should have warned her the first time that I was hooding her instead of simply throwing the cover over her head. Admittedly, a wrong move on my part, but it had been instinctive since I'd done it countless times on terrorists we'd captured and brought back to base.

"I can't take you back until Viktor releases Marcus. The cops might be staking your house and I can't risk it."

It was two in the morning and I wasn't taking any chances.

"So, I'm your prisoner."

I gripped the steering wheel. "Yup."

"Can you at least tell me if Marcus's going to be okay?"

"Such concern for the commander." I couldn't keep the bite from my tone.

"He didn't look okay."

I clamped my mouth shut because I was afraid I might lash out at her. I concentrated on driving instead of dealing with a wife who didn't want to be my wife anymore. Who showed more concern for someone else other than me, her husband, who she hadn't seen in three years. Three years where my every waking moment was thoughts of her. And each time I closed my eyes to sleep? It was her face I saw.

What a mindfuck.

The silence in the car was choking, and I was relieved to see the exit coming up.

"Drake?"

"Not now," I bit out.

"Why are you mad?"

"Think on that for a minute."

"Are you being sarcastic?"

Jesus Christ.

She huffed in her seat and, out of the corner of my eye, I saw her look out the window. I resisted the urge to speed down the ramp leading to the house I'd rented, but the surging adrenaline in my system needed its own outlet; I just didn't know where. I was afraid I might take it out on Izabel. Being alone with her was not a good idea at the moment, but I had no choice. She had to stay out of the public eye and there was no one I trusted to be her security.

The house that Hank found for me was on a thousand-acre rural development. Horse fences lined the roadway, until, finally, we came upon the stone columns that marked the property entrance. I was gratified to hear the catch in Izabel's breathing as we drove through the subdivision. The full moon was high, and it spilled its light on the sprawling meadows. A large part of the acreage remained untouched to give the residents privacy and the country-estate flair.

The Escalade turned onto a paved driveway where it stopped in front of an all-brick Georgian house.

"I packed some of your clothes," I told her. When I exited the vehicle, Izabel did the same, but her eyes were riveted on the house. After getting the overnight bags from the back, I slammed the tailgate and walked up beside her. Landscaping lights illuminated the front of the house and the covered porch.

"Why?" She turned to face me, her eyes suspiciously glassy.

"I wanted to remind you of what we once had."

"By throwing one of my designs back in my face?"

"That was not my intention." Her reaction bewildered me. I was at a loss at what to do anymore. Nothing made her happy. Maybe she was right—I'd changed; she'd changed, too.

Frustration constricted my chest. I refused to accept defeat.

I unlocked the heavy door and threw it open. The foyer chandelier was already on and it didn't take me long to find the other switches to flood the house with light. It had a beautiful interior, one I knew Izabel would appreciate, but she was seething.

"Do you remember what we used to do?" I dropped the bags on the floor and moved into her space. Not waiting for her answer, I continued, "On the weekends—because *my wife* was such a workaholic—we'd fill up our coffee mugs and drive to some of your projects. We'd each point out what we liked and what we wanted to go into our dream house." Her eyes grew distant as if remembering. A telltale smile softened her lips, so I pressed on. "You lost interest in our routine months before my deployment and I didn't know why."

Her gaze dropped to the floor. I bent over and unzipped one of the duffels and extracted crumpled sheets of vellum.

When she saw what was in my hand, big tears rolled from the corners of her eyes.

"I found this in the trash can of your office," I said softly. "I checked the date. It was the month I left." Sorrow clogged the words in my throat, but I got them out. "Three years ago."

Izabel opened her mouth, and her breath hitched in a soundless cry. Tears fell faster and she shook her head. "You had no right to go through my trash."

"You lost interest because you'd already designed our dream house—"

"Stop!" she yelled. "Why don't you just stop!" Her eyes flared angrily. "We can't go back to what we used to be—"

I dropped the ruined plans of the house and grabbed her shoulders. "Tell me why. Why won't you even try?" I thought of the architect after her. "Is it because of that man?"

"What man?"

"The one who kissed you!"

"Kyle?" Hearing his name snapped the last threads of my control. Rage hazed my vision and, before I realized what I was doing, I grabbed Izabel by her ass. Lifting her, I walked us toward the dining table.

"What are you doing?" she cried. "Put me down!"

I dropped her on the table and slammed my mouth on hers in a ferocious, claiming kiss. The need to erase the other man's touch was all-consuming. Izabel was fucking mine.

She struggled, but I was unrelenting. My hand curled around her nape. I plundered her lips, forcing them open, our lips clashing as my tongue swept inside, uncaring if she bit me. Wanting to feel her skin, I yanked at the front of her sweater, scattering buttons. My greedy hand left her nape and delved behind the cup of her bra while the other unhooked it. The feeling of her nipple taut against my palm made me so goddamn hard.

She moaned into my mouth, beginning to respond, and I coaxed her further into complete surrender.

She was hanging off the table now, one arm wrapped around my neck as she rubbed her pussy against my erection. Her hand slipped beneath my shirt, stroking my abs. I rumbled in approval.

I needed her taste on my tongue.

I loathed breaking our connection, but I murmured for her to kick off her sneakers and she quickly complied. Then I laid her down on the table, bending over her, capturing her nipple with my tongue, before I planted kisses down her rib cage, all the while pulling her leggings down.

Her arousal hit my nose. If anything, we had this.

I could work with this. Win back her love, her trust.

"Drake…"

"Shh…I've got you, baby."

"I…Oh, God."

I buried my face between her legs, pushing her underwear aside, and tasted sweet heaven. Her legs convulsed around my head as I continued to eat her, savor her, sucking her clit, diving into a honeysuckle sweetness I'd missed for three years. Her cries of pleasure pierced the room, only fueling the thrust of my tongue inside her.

Her fingers gripped my hair as her hips bucked against my mouth. I prolonged her orgasm. When her legs relaxed on my back, I eased up and swiped my tongue over my mouth, certain it was glistening with her juices.

Undoing my zipper, I gave relief to my raging erection that couldn't wait to be sucked into her heat. But first I was going to kiss her slow and sweet. I bent over her when a suppressed sob made me pause.

A chilled fist squeezed my heart.

"Iza?"

"Not like this," she choked between sobs, the back of her hand over her mouth. "Not like this."

My erection deflated as her despair threw cold water over my lust. Izabel pushed up on her elbows, pulling on her torn sweater to cover herself up. Sorrow streamed down her cheeks, making me feel like shit.

She didn't want me? Had I misread her response? I tucked myself back into my jeans and zipped up.

I stared at her, helpless at the face of her tears.

"Not like this," she repeated for a third time. "I'm attracted to you." Her slender throat bobbed. "My body knows you. It can't say no even when my mind and my heart are screaming to stop." Heaving sharply to control her emotions, she expelled a long sigh, before she raised anguish-filled eyes that made me flinch. "But I want to be sure. If you take me now, we'll be reducing our marriage to a one-night stand. Because this"—she pointed between the two of us—"is what it will feel like."

Her words cut through me as sharp as my KA-BAR blade severing my carotid artery. I bled. My mind, body, and heart belonged to her and only her, and it gutted me she didn't feel the same.

"Three years...I fought my way back to you, Izabel, but I'm drowning here. I want my wife back." I lifted an arm and let it drop in a hopeless gesture. "Deep inside, I know it's a me problem. I have to give you time to adjust to my return. I don't know what else to do. But I can't be the only one fighting. For us to stand a chance, you need to let go of this resentment for me, for what I've done. You need to fight for us, too." Pain throbbed deep within the marrow of my bones. "I can't walk away from you because I've done nothing but fight to get back to you." *Jesus, I'm rambling in circles.* "You need time. I get it. But in the meantime, this"—I pointed between us just as she had done earlier—"is destroying me."

I said my piece. There was nothing left for me to say or do. I didn't expect to snap my fingers and everything would be fixed, but it was who I was. Her husband. I didn't know how to be anyone else.

I looked at the stairs beyond her shoulders. "The main bedroom is on the second floor. If you prefer a smaller room, mine is the next one over."

I backed away from her slowly. Alarm crossed her face.

"Where are you going?"

"I need"—I vented a shaky breath—"to clear my head."

"Drake?"

I ignored her pleading tone and headed for the door.

"Drake!"

I refused to turn around. I refused to break down in front of her. I wanted it all, not the crumbs she would give me out of pity.

I didn't want her pity.

The yearning inside me threatened to send me to my knees. I yanked the door open and slammed it behind me.

chapter **twelve**

Izabel

I rushed to the foyer, barefoot and naked except for my ruined sweater and panties. The devastation on Drake's face triggered visceral emotions deep inside me. Emotions I couldn't name, but they compelled me to follow him. They prevented me from letting him walk away like this. So broken. Like he'd already lost me.

My hand circled the doorknob but froze when I heard him roar.

A guttural, plaintive howl that shredded my insides, releasing the familiar emotions from my heart that I'd kept locked down since his return. Yes, bounded by resentment and anger. Drake was right. But was I so wrong? I understood our disconnect. Of course I did. He'd had years knowing he'd return to me while I had years trying to move on from him.

We were on opposing ends of emotions and expectations.

My hand dropped from the knob, and I turned from the door, leaning against it. I'd never heard such agonizing sounds come out of my husband.

Eyes blurring, I slid to the floor as my pain streamed down my cheeks. Losing Drake, the days when I thought I couldn't go on. The resolve that held me together during my three-month prenatal checkup only to have that ripped away from me when I lost our baby weeks later.

I clawed out of my grief, channeled all my energy and time into making other people's lives better. Did I have the fortitude to be with a man like Drake again?

That was the root of my problem.

Fear.

My head throbbed with indecision. Plus, I hadn't fully recovered from the tranquilizer effects, and this confrontation with Drake was draining.

Eyes drooping, I let myself go.

Someone was carrying me.

"Drake?" I mumbled.

"Sleep, baby." A gravelly voice spoke to me. "I've got you."

I snuggled into the safety of his embrace.

I awakened to the smell of coffee and unfamiliar surroundings. Roman shades blocked the sunlight, but starbursts rimmed their edges. A gold jacquard divan sat below the window ledge. The walls were painted a dusky blue.

Carefully, I peeked under the comforter, confused that I was in my nightshirt. Then flashes of the night before hit me.

Drake ripping my sweater apart.

Drake kissing me senseless.

Drake burying his face between my thighs.

Heat shot up my face into the roots of my hair. I groaned into my pillow. "I am such a slut."

One kiss. Dammit. One kiss and I ignited. My body was such a traitor and I surrendered to the strings of its master. Our physical chemistry was undeniable, undimmed by the years, it seemed, but was it enough to risk my heart again?

Tossing back the covers, I lowered my feet to the plush carpet and noticed an open duffel sitting by the divan. Nothing had changed. Drake was bossy, as always, and took it upon himself to pack for me. But we both knew how to pick our battles. This was why we had such a successful marriage when divorce among our peers was at an all-time high.

A cylinder of rolled-up vellum paper sat on top of the bag.

They were the plans of our dream house, which I had crumpled and thrown in the trash the day I went on a date with Kyle. White marks left permanent cracks in the design and reminded me of the state of my marriage. Drake's words last night about hanging on to my anger came echoing back. If I let go, we could begin again just as I could draw a new house plan on a pristine sheet of vellum.

I looked around for my purse. It was nowhere in the room. Damn secret agent stuff. They didn't want me calling anyone. I wouldn't be surprised if my husband had done something to it so it wasn't trackable.

I needed answers.

After taking care of my morning routine, thankful that Drake remembered how meticulous I was with my skin care products, I surveyed myself in the mirror. My lids were puffy from crying but, somehow, our encounter last night had been cathartic. Or maybe I was relieved that even though my heart and mind were confused, there was still a part of me that responded to Drake. A part of me that still wanted to be his wife again.

I returned to the bedroom and looked through the bag for something to wear. I pulled out a pair of jeans and a hoodie. My chest twitched when I spotted my slip-on shoes.

There was little Drake had forgotten about me.

When I stepped out of the bedroom, I absorbed the familiar layout of the second floor. A sweeping staircase separated the two wings of the house. There was a room next to mine and one at the far end of the hallway. The opposite wing had an upstairs parlor and two more rooms. This was similar to our dream house, except I made better use of the center stairway, which would open to the family room.

"Ugh," I berated myself for reminiscing about a time that would only bring me heartache. I could not, should not, relapse into the shell of the woman I'd been. My anticipation of seeing a bare-chested Drake was not helping either. But when I cleared the last step and turned into the kitchen, there was no sign of him.

Instead, a woman who appeared to be in her late fifties sat at the breakfast nook, sipping coffee as she casually swiped across her tablet.

"Uhm...good morning?" I couldn't help the questioning tone that crept into my voice.

The woman glanced up and smiled serenely. "Morning, Izabel."

Cautiously stepping into the breakfast nook, I swiped my hands at my sides before shoving them into my back pockets as I waited for the woman to say something.

"I'm Gina Carter," the woman said as she rose and held out her hand.

Despite my reservation, I returned the courtesy. "Where's Drake?"

"He'll join us later."

"Us?" This time I eyed the older woman suspiciously. "Who exactly are you?"

"A friend."

Eyes further narrowing, I crossed my arms. "Try again."

Gina noted my defensive movement with a faint smile. "I'm Drake's therapist."

A psychiatrist. I lowered my arms and spun away slightly, shaking my head in disbelief. "Unbelievable."

When Gina didn't respond, I faced her again. "How can Drake...how can you expect me to talk to you"—I snapped my fingers—"just like that."

The older woman's eyes reflected compassion and I bristled in consternation.

"We weren't expecting you to agree—"

"Do I look like I need an intervention?" I challenged. "It's only been a few days."

Gina sat back in her chair. "It's more like Drake needs me

to intervene. Apparently he's doing a poor job at this reconciliation."

"Understatement," I mumbled under my breath. "And his answer is to have me open up to a complete stranger?"

"Sometimes a stranger is better to be a sounding board."

I laughed derisively. "Except that's not true for you, is it? You probably have preconceived notions of me already."

"I understand your outrage." The other woman nodded. "Do you trust Drake?"

I didn't respond.

"I didn't think so," Gina said. "What about Hank?"

"What about him?"

"If he vouches for me, would you agree to speak to me?"

I blew out a resigned breath. "I don't know who to trust anymore, even Hank, because he saw me spiraling, yet knew Drake was alive. No one. No one is really on my side."

"I'm sorry, Izabel. I really am. But given the special nature of your situation with Drake, we can't just bring in another mediator."

"So you work for the CIA."

"I'm retired," Gina said. "But I used to work for the agency."

The woman before me looked like a spinster aunt. An elegant spinster aunt.

Gina spread her hands in a glib gesture. "Unfortunately, marital strife is not my specialty, so I'll try my best here."

"I haven't agreed to talk to you."

The shrink smiled faintly before picking up her phone and swiping the screen. She put the phone on speaker.

After a few rings, Hank's voice came on the line. "Our boy crash and burn?"

Gina laughed briefly. "You can say that."

"I don't need a shrink," I declared.

"I agree, but you need someone to explain where Drake is coming from because I doubt he has the tact or words to express himself," Hank said. "I've seen you both go through hell..." He paused. "You tried to move on, Izzy, but I know you. You still love Drake. And, sweetie, he loves you more than anything. You're feeling betrayed, but don't deny yourself the chance to see where this can go."

"Well, hell, I don't know if I'm needed here," Gina interjected with amusement.

"Sorry, Doc G." Hank chuckled. "You get me, Izzy?"

"Goodness," I exclaimed. "It's only been four days—"

He laughed. "It's Maddox we're talking about here."

I had to smile. Yes, Drake wasn't a very patient man, especially when it came to me. Somehow, I wasn't surprised at the speed my husband wanted to get back in my life. My foremost reservation was the fear that I would never become the SEAL wife I used to be. I no longer wanted the uncertainty and the sacrifice of being kept in the dark about what my husband was doing.

I'd paid that price. Still, the boundaries or our reconciliation could be up for discussion. But Gina, as Drake's therapist, could fill in the blanks and put in perspective what he could never open up about. His vulnerability when he was injured and the guilt that must have consumed him when he faked his death and left me to grieve him.

I sighed in resignation. "Okay." I looked at Gina. "But if I'm feeling manipulated, we're done."

"Told you she was a tough chick."

"Yes, Maddox schooled me."

"I'm getting coffee," I grumbled. "Talk to you soon, Hank." I headed for the coffee machine and wondered what I had agreed to. There was comfort knowing Hank was onboard with Gina getting involved, but it didn't mean it had gotten rid of my reservations.

Stirring milk into my coffee, I turned and leaned against the counter and locked eyes with Gina. "Just so you know, I've had enough therapy and grief counseling to last me a lifetime. They built me back up to what I am now. I'm not perfect. I have my scars. I'm not going to stand for one of those sessions where you break me down in order to build me up."

"I'm not in psy-ops," Gina said, amused. "I don't handle the brainwashing part."

There's a brainwashing part?

Gina turned in her seat to face me. She crossed her legs and leaned back in her chair. "I'm not really certain that division exists. My job at the agency is to ensure the effectiveness of an asset."

"At all costs, I presume."

Gina couldn't miss the sarcasm in my voice. "Yes. But we're not here to talk about me."

"Let's get this over with."

"All right." The other woman leaned forward. "Tell me about your mother."

THE MORNING PASSED, but Gina had not once asked about Drake. Over a breakfast of croissants and coffee, I told her about my mother, Carmen Rodriguez. I had fond memories of Ma.

"She had a flair for styling hair and applying makeup," I said proudly. "She was in demand for weddings and photo shoots."

"She never thought to open her own salon?"

"No. She preferred to rent space, to be her own boss without a lot of overhead."

"And your father?"

Sadness tweaked my heart and I studied the bottom of my coffee mug. "He wasn't in the picture. Ma loved with all her heart, but she kept falling for the wrong men." I glanced at Gina. "She had a brief affair with my father who was a married man."

"Ouch."

"Yup. When she got pregnant, he wanted her to have an abortion. My mother was horrified, not only because she was Catholic, but that she could have fallen for such a man. The rose-colored glasses came off quickly, and she kicked him to the curb."

Gina nodded as if filing the information away. "You got into an Ivy League school for college?"

"My mother was a proud woman. She never accepted a dime from my father, but she broke her wrist at an inopportune time when she'd made poor investments and she lost most of our savings." I shook my head at the memory. "I was in my third year of high school and our house was under threat of foreclosure. She approached my father."

"Have you ever met him?"

"He doesn't want to meet me." I shrugged. "I've long accepted it."

"You know who he is, though?"

"Yes," I sighed. "He's from a political dynasty in the Midwest. Old money. His wife is old money too. Ma didn't feel guilty about blackmailing him to get me into Cornell. She said it was years of child support and my father was running for governor."

"Perfect timing." Gina chuckled.

"It was."

"She wasn't afraid that your father could send someone to silence her? That was risky."

My mother was a contrary woman. "She didn't say it. But she believed my father truly loved her."

"And when she asked for the money?"

"He didn't think twice. I think it was because he loved my mother, but he loved his political career more."

"Why do you say that?"

"Ma died a year after I graduated."

"So she met Drake?"

Hearing his name spurred a wariness that changed the tone of our conversation from easy nostalgia to the purpose of this meeting. *Well played, Doc G.*

"Yes, she did, albeit only briefly. She had lung cancer. And no, she wasn't a smoker. Her oncologist thought it was from her years of cleaning houses and the exposure to the chemicals." My heart ached at my mother's sacrifices. "The chemicals at the salon didn't help either, but it was too late."

"She loved what she was doing at the end, though, right?" Gina said.

"She did." I puffed out a brave breath to keep from crying. "Anyway, I visited my mother's gravesite the week after her burial, and there was a single white rose at the headstone."

"You think it was from your father?"

"I know it was. Every year on the day of her death, there is one perfect rose."

A contemplative pause hung between us.

"Hmm..." Gina steepled her fingers over her coffee cup. "You don't seem to have abandonment fears or daddy issues. Your mother raised a strong, self-confident woman and, from what Drake told me, you handled his deployments well."

"It wasn't easy, but I knew what I signed up for when I married him."

"I don't need to remind you how tough it is for SEALs and their spouses to stay together," Gina said dryly. She checked her watch. "I think we've talked enough for this morning. How about we take a break and take a walk on the grounds? It's a gorgeous neighborhood."

"A couple of my designs were optioned by the builders in this subdivision."

"More like an estate community." Gina rose from her chair. "Shall we?"

It wasn't the brain-draining or grueling therapy session I'd been expecting. Remembering my mother reminded me of the strength she'd instilled inside me. I didn't know what Gina was up to, but I was up for more.

IT WAS LATER in the afternoon over tea and sweet biscuits when Gina made her move.

We began with a baking session. The shrink had a penchant for French sweets and suggested baking madeleines. Surprised, I watched her unearth an antique madeleine baking tin and a hand-held mixer from her shopping bag. This was followed by the requisite dry ingredients. Then she walked to the refrigerator and pulled out the butter and eggs needed for this traditional small cake of northeastern France.

I wasn't complaining. I loved baking. Drake's favorite was the tres leches cake. A recipe Ma passed down to me. Buttery fragrance permeated the air of the kitchen and wrapped around my heart like a comforting blanket. There was no doubt the walk and the baking exercise were part of Gina's efforts to put me at ease.

When the madeleines were done and Gina suggested we partake of all our hard-earned work in the sunroom, my guard slammed up again, though not as closed off as it had been when we'd first met.

This time Gina brewed tea to go with the sweets.

The shrink smiled as she poured me a cup. "It's Midnight Lychee. Nothing to worry about. Nothing mind-altering in it."

"Sorry." I did look suspiciously at Gina for a minute there.

I also tried not to swoon too much when the first bite of the petite cake melted on my tongue. Still, I couldn't help gushing. "Ohmigod." I swiped my mouth with a finger to keep a crumb from falling. "This is so good."

Gina's eyes clouded and she gave a small smile. "It was my daughter's favorite."

Was?

I finished the cake and took a sip of tea, forcing a smile when I looked back at her. "Was?"

"I had a daughter, Bobbi. She was eleven." Gina picked up a sugar cube and dropped it into her tea and stirred. "She loved flowers, baby goats, and sweets. She loved running barefoot in the dirt and climbing trees. But the one thing she loved the most was baking with her gram." She nodded to the plate of madeleines. "My mother was French and that's her antique tin I inherited from my grandmother." Gina's eyes grew glassy. "I had hoped to pass it on to Bobbi." Giving one shake of her head, she continued. "We never thought Bobbi would have such a severe allergic reaction to bee stings. She'd been stung before and the swelling wasn't much. That summer, my husband and I took a much-needed vacation and left Bobbi with my mother on her farm. She wandered off into the woods, which was something she always did anyway. We believe she'd stumbled upon a beehive."

I found myself reaching out to Gina, covering the other woman's hand that was wrapped around her teacup.

"You don't have to tell me this," I whispered. "I understand why you are, but…"

"Bobbi's death broke our family," Gina said. "My mom blamed herself. My husband blamed me, and our marriage didn't survive. I'm a psychiatrist and yet I couldn't help the people around me because my grief made it difficult to see theirs. Eventually, my mother forgave herself. I never blamed her...but I lost her there for a while." Gina flipped the hand I was holding and clasped ours together. She looked me straight in the eye. "I think Drake's return yanked the bottom bricks from the foundation you've built to move on from him and your baby's loss."

Talons of anguish clawed up my throat, making it difficult to speak. I nodded rapidly instead, controlling the tremble in my lips. Exhaling raggedly, I said, "Knowing I was pregnant helped me hang on to that last thread of sanity. Losing the baby and Drake within months of each other was almost too much to bear..." I gulped back a sob. "There were so many times I prayed to God to take me as well..." My voice trailed off. "Why didn't he just take me so I could be with Drake and our baby?"

"Oh, Izabel."

"You're right in a way. All my grief, all the strength I drew within myself to survive had become a joke. I was consoling myself that Drake left a part of him with me when he died, and then I lost our daughter."

Resentment scratched close to the surface of my skin. "Now I'm angry at him for not being there when I needed him the most." I withdrew my hand from Gina's, crossing my arms and hugging my biceps, wanting to disappear into myself like the many times I retreated from life when the pain became too much to comprehend. "I also feel guilt for not being supportive of the sacrifices he's made. I knew he thought it was what was best for us. My mind is telling me he did the right thing, but I can't help what I feel, you know?"

"Like he abandoned you?"

"Yes. I married a SEAL. I understood what I was taking on and yet he didn't trust me enough to share the burden with him. That's why it makes me so mad that he did this to me... to us."

"He was desperate to return to you," Gina said softly. "He'd hit rock bottom when I met him. His injuries were severe and he'd spent days going out of his mind thinking about what he was putting you through…"

"He should have found another way. I would have gone into hiding with him."

"He didn't have much choice then."

"He told me and…I should understand him." Tears scalded my eyes. "But it hurts too much and I'm afraid to be his wife again."

Understanding showed through the other woman's eyes. "If it makes any difference…when he found out you lost the baby, he was determined to come home to you."

"Then why didn't he?!" I rasped.

"They shot him with a tranquilizer and kept him locked in a room for days," the shrink stated baldly.

"What?" Outrage fired through every fiber of my being; it was the feeling of outrage of a wife for her husband. "How could they? After all that he had been through?"

Gina sighed. "I'd prefer it if you didn't tell him I told you that. The last thing Drake wants from you is pity. But I felt you should know, when it came down to it, Drake chose you."

"But…" Still reeling from this bit of information, I looked everywhere until I forced myself to focus on the teapot in front of me. Drake was a proud man. He wouldn't use pity to get me back. But Gina's revelation chipped away at my fear and awakened an ache…a fire to fight for our marriage.

"Tell me honestly. Do you think there's hope for Drake and me?"

"Yes," Gina answered without hesitation. "I have no doubt about Drake's determination to win you back. That man isn't a quitter and you need to experience his devotion on your own. I can't tell you that. I've seen his strength and now I'm beginning to understand yours. I'm optimistic."

"So, as our therapist, what do you suggest should be our next steps?"

chapter
thirteen

IZABEL

FOR TWO DAYS after my first meeting with Doc G, Drake gave me lots of space during the day. I wasn't naïve to think I was truly alone. The entire property was probably wired, and either Hank or the Guardians were keeping an eye on me. Drake came home in the afternoon, always with a paper bag of my favorite food and an orchid.

I smiled, staring at the two new orchids below the picture window.

The first night it was Indian food—butter chicken—and a Cattleya orchid. The second evening, Drake picked up shrimp lo-mein. Surprisingly, the orchid that day was a Cymbidium. It wasn't a common orchid, even in typical greenhouses, so my husband must have contacted an orchid enthusiast.

Drake's attempts at good old-fashioned courtship pleased me. Somehow, it was a way for us to reconnect, to ease me back into the romantic part of our marriage. Still, this isolation bothered me. I shared with Drake how worried I was about the repercussions of my disappearance. Drake assured me it wouldn't be long now, and that Marcus and I would soon return to the public eye.

The conversation between us began to lose its awkwardness. He was feeling less like a stranger and more like the man I used to know. My husband. It was time to reveal that one piece of information I'd kept close to my heart. I talked to Hank on the phone I could use and discovered that Drake never knew about my secret. It was mine to share, Hank said, when the right time came.

"Iza?"

Drake's voice followed the closing of the front door. I hurried down the stairs, dressed in jeans, a sweater, and sneakers.

"Going somewhere?" His brows furrowed.

"Yes."

"Iza, we can't be seen in public."

"I know." My smile was small and tentative. "But trust me?" I held out my hand.

His frown cleared, replaced by a look of hope. As for me, my heart expanded with what felt like the love I'd always had for him.

It was time for healing.

Wrought-iron gates and moss-covered columns loomed before us. My heart contracted with that familiar ache whenever I visited this somber place. It was a cloudy day. Fall had painted the trees in gold, rust, and orange, giving color to a land dotted with tombstones. Drake stiffened beside me and I heard his sharp inhale, but not the release of his breath.

"Why are we here, Iza?" His voice was rough as he guided the Escalade through the cemetery gates.

"It's time for you to meet her," I said softly. Tears scalded my eyes, but I kept them at bay because, once the floodgates opened, there was no stopping its torrent and there was so much to say. My words were garbled as I added, "Over there." I pointed up the road to a small hill that held the plots of the children's cemetery.

A shudder and a ragged exhale shook the man beside me, but I kept my gaze forward. I needn't look at Drake to see the devastation on his face, because that was the same expression I'd seen reflected in the mirror for countless days in the past three years.

"Stop here."

The SUV rolled to a halt. I pushed the door open and hopped out. Drake's own door opened and closed, but I didn't hear any footsteps. I angled to him, and a sob hitched in my throat.

Drake's face was mottled with a ruddy color, as if all the blood had gone to his head. Tears streamed down his face, and his mouth was slightly parted, trembling, as he'd been trying to hold back his own tears.

"Drake?" I reached out my hand. "It's time to meet Angelise."

. . .

THE TREK to our daughter's little grave was a blur. The marble headstone gleamed amidst the smell of newly turned earth. When we reached the spot, Drake collapsed to his knees with his head bowed, his shoulders shaking with the force of his silent sobs. His breath occasionally caught as he dragged air into his lungs. My own cheeks were wet but, at the moment, I was the strong one as I knelt beside my husband and hugged him. He leaned into my embrace and I hoped I gave him comfort.

Finally, our healing began.

ANGELINA ELISE MADDOX
Beloved daughter
Heaven has gained an angel

IT WAS over twenty minutes before our tears subsided.

"You named her after Nan," Drake said, tracing the engraved letters *Elise* on the headstone.

"You had such admiration for your grandmother, I thought it was fitting. I nicknamed her Angelise—a combination of both names."

Drake continued to inhale sharply and exhale shudderingly slow, trying to control the flood of emotions that must be overwhelming him.

"Hello, little one." His voice cracked, and he blinked, a tear catching on his thick lashes. I was in danger of falling apart. I'd always known him as my protective husband. The warrior SEAL. I'd never seen him this vulnerable before. I'd never seen him cry like this. Even the strongest of men could be driven to their knees with the devastating loss of a child. I suspected Drake had never truly mourned our daughter until now.

After a while, he switched his gaze from the headstone to me as though waiting for me to say something.

"Burying a husband and a daughter within months of each other...there were so many times I wanted to die, too," I began. "When I lost Angelise, the emptiness inside me wasn't only physical, it was as if I'd lost who I was...as if I'd become this non-entity. It scared me—this gaping black abyss inside me. I had nightmares that a pit of tar was swallowing me whole and I would cry out for you to help me." Drake winced, but I stilled myself because it needed to be said. "I called out for you. At times, I thought I could hear your voice, but then you weren't there and I would feel like dying all over again. "

"I'm sorry, Iza."

I nodded. "I just want you to understand why I was so angry at you when you came back alive and well. Why I felt betrayed. We made vows to each other and, when I needed you the most, you weren't there." Drake was shaking his head...in regret? But he didn't say anything. "Doc G asked me an important question. And that was whether knowing the man you are, if there was a chance of happiness for us if you didn't go after your team's killers."

He froze.

I cupped his face in the cradle of my palms to keep our gazes locked. "The man I love has integrity and would never rest until he brings those murderers to justice." I searched his eyes. "If you came back, we would be living half a life. We couldn't be truly happy. A part of your soul was lost when your team died. My question is, Drake, have you gotten that missing part back?"

"I'm almost there, Iza," he said softly. The love reflected in his slate-blue irises left no doubt that it was me who would finally complete him.

chapter
fourteen

DRAKE

I DROVE the Escalade into the four-car garage of the estate home and turned off its engine. I grabbed the Italian takeout bag and another orchid I'd picked up on the way home.

Doc G had called me an hour before to let me know she was leaving. It was Izabel's second meeting with the shrink and three days after that cathartic scene at Angelise's grave. At first, I was pissed that I didn't know more about her, but my anger quickly dissipated when Izabel held out her hand, asking me to meet our daughter.

It was as if all my guilt over abandoning my family had finally found its place in the past. When we returned to the house that night, our dynamics shifted, the last barrier keeping us apart evaporated. Were we fixed? Of course not, but hope shined like a beacon in a storm-tossed ocean because my wife was starting to look at me in the way she used to—with love and adoration.

During the day, I cooled my heels at Castle Rock, sitting beside Tim as I assisted Edmunds and Brick in their stakeout of Allison Tierney. We also discussed how to spin our story and return Izabel and Marcus to society after their "alleged" kidnapping by the notorious gang. Viktor was of the mind to use my back-from-the-dead story as bait and see what rats we could trap. As Tierney was the chief of staff of a possible future president, we needed to act fast and figure out if her boss was complicit.

I opened the door of the garage leading into the house. "Iza?"

The kitchen had the under-cabinet lights on and a faint smell of toasted butter permeated the air. They'd been baking madeleines again.

I smiled.

I tracked movement from the living room, and that was where I saw her.

"Here." Izabel rose from the couch, a tablet in hand. She was wearing a short tee and low-riding drawstring gray sweatpants. Her heavy tits conformed to her tight top, and her belly button was exposed. My heart somersaulted beneath my chest. A stirring in my groin didn't bode well for my self-control tonight. Jesus, what was this woman doing? Izabel knew how much I loved her exposed belly button, and all I wanted to do was throw her on the couch, rip away her clothes, and fuck her.

I was like an ex-con who hadn't had a woman in years.

A knowing smile played on Izabel's lips.

Oh, my little temptress.

"Everything go well today?" My voice croaked. I lowered the takeout and orchid on the dining table.

"It did." She closed the distance between us and trailed a finger down my torso. My abs tightened in response. "How hungry are you?"

Every muscle in my body seized, and I forced myself to put our relationship above my lust, but I had to be honest. "I don't want to mess this up—"

"I wasn't suggesting sex."

Just that three-letter word out of her mouth conjured up all the erotic images in my head.

She bit her lower lip. "I don't want to mess this up either." Izabel was fair-skinned enough that a blush on her was discernible. At that moment, though, her face was flaming. "Uhm, I was thinking." Her eyes lowered to my crotch, widened, and then quickly returned to my eyes.

I smirked.

"Stop that," she whispered.

"Am I making you uncomfortable?"

"Not in the way you mean."

"Maybe it's exactly the way I want it to mean."

"Drake…" she chided in gentle annoyance.

"Iza…" I teased.

She puffed a short laugh. She was adorable and I wanted to snatch her in my arms. Fuck, this was torture.

"So what's on your mind besides eating this delicious Italian dinner I brought home?"

She looked at me critically. "Do you still use a straight-edge razor?"

"Hell yeah." I grinned, beginning to see where she was going with this.

"Have it with you?"

"Yup."

"Then let's give you a shave and a haircut."

"Gina suggested we engage in a familiar activity that's also personal," Izabel said as she tested the sharpness of the razor on a section of my hair. She used to cut my hair and sometimes gave me a shave. "I kinda like this longish style on you. Mind if I trim a bit?"

I shrugged. "Whatever you want, baby."

We were in the main bedroom. Izabel told me to take a shower, so it'd be easier for her to give me a haircut. Meanwhile I sat on a swivel stool that was part of the vanity table with only a towel wrapped around my waist. My oversized frame probably looked ridiculous on it, but I didn't care. Izabel was behind me, running her fingers through my scalp, and, if I were a cat, I'd be purring right now.

Holding out a section, she shaved off the edges. Clumps of hair fell to the tiled floor as awareness and heat flicked against my skin with every brush of her body against mine. My cock began to tent the towel and I forced myself to think of Brick in a pink dress because it made me more squeamish than thinking of blood and guts. I played this game with my erection while Izabel moved temptingly around me.

"Do you like this length?" Her eyes met mine in the mirror.

"Looks good to me."

"Great," she breathed and situated herself in front of me. I widened my legs to allow her to move between them, the towel precariously gaping open. A hitch in her breathing told me she was as affected as I was. She worked on trimming my beard. Our eyes met briefly. I fought the urge to steal a kiss, and I didn't want the razor to slice my cheek open either.

Staying as still as a statue was a great fucking idea.

After Izabel finished, she moved back behind me and cupped my jaw. "I'm gonna work on your beard line."

I chuckled. "You don't have to."

"Oh, but I want to." She smeared shaving gel on my cheek.

"Want to find your husband beneath the scruff?"

"You can say that. Now, hush before I cut you."

I closed my mouth, because the back of my head was more or less cradled on her tits.

Fuck.

Torture. Fucking sweet torture.

I squeezed my eyes shut.

Brick in a skirt.

Brick in a tutu.

Fuck. It wasn't working.

Izabel released my jaw and backed away. A warm, wet towel wiped the gel from my face.

I opened my eyes and stared at my reflection—and recognized a man I hadn't seen in three years. My eyes shifted to Izabel's and the watery smile on her face told me what I needed to know—my wife had found her husband.

"Drake…"

A growl escaped my throat as I swiveled on the stool and

grabbed her hips. Her laughter was cut short when I lifted her and planted her ass on the counter. The towel falling away exposed my fully erect cock.

Izabel's hand wrapped around my throbbing erection.

"Fuck, Izabel." My eyes drilled into her fevered ones. "Are you sure?"

Her "yes" was needy, and I was a slave to her every need.

I framed her face and kissed her, devouring her lips like a man starved. Our tongues tangled. I was acutely aware of her soft hands stroking my cock and squeezing.

I knocked her hands away. "Enough."

She protested and tried to grab me again, but I foiled her attempt.

"Too much," I growled. I yanked at the drawstrings of her sweatpants as she took off her shirt. I stripped it off her legs and moved between them again, pressing close. Claiming her lips, I dug a hand behind her underwear.

Hot. Wet.

I plunged a finger inside her and she moaned into my mouth.

"Fuck, Iza." I trailed kisses down her neck and slipped off the strap of her bra so I could devour her gorgeous tits. I swallowed a nipple, sucking and licking as a second finger joined the first. She was fucking tight as her slick inner muscles suctioned my fingers.

"Inside me, Drake!" she whimpered.

I looked up from eating her tit—"don't rush me"—and resumed feasting on her body. She cried out as she came on my fingers and I continued to wring out every shudder of her orgasm as I lavished her skin with attention. I couldn't wait to taste her, to have her juices on my tongue.

I plucked her from the counter and her legs automatically wrapped around me. Walking to the still-dark bedroom, I planted a knee on the bed and dropped her ass near the edge of the mattress. My knees hit the floor and I yanked her panties.

"Spread." I shoved her thighs apart and dove in, tongue lapping greedily, the taste of her cunt turning my cock rock hard. Izabel squirmed as I tongue-fucked her. I brought her to the brink, withdrew, and then took her to new heights.

"Drake."

I recognized that keening moan, relished that I still knew my wife's pleasure points, how to drive her mad with need and bring her to orgasm.

I sucked on her clit.

"Drake!" And there it was. The explosion I was dying to taste. Her wet heat coated my mouth and I swiped every drop. Crawling up her body, I began pressing the crown of my cock inside her.

She was going to be tight and I didn't want to hurt her.

"Let me know if it's too much, baby," I whispered to her in the dark, seeing the gleam in her eyes, but not her clear features. The bathroom fixture was our only source of light.

I continued to inch in. "Okay?" I gritted. Jesus, her pussy was tight.

She nodded vigorously, but her eyes squeezed shut.

Shit. Was that pain? Pleasure? I started to withdraw.

"No!" Her ankles hooked behind my ass, locking me in place.

I slid home, anchoring myself to the hilt.

"Fuck, you feel so good," I groaned. I struggled not to rut into her like a deranged beast and, instead, stayed planted. I needed to see her. Staying connected, I shifted us until I could see Izabel's face in the dim light. Her blissful smile made my heart soar. I was getting my wife back. I pressed gentle kisses all over her face before capturing her lips in a deep, searing one.

"I love you, Izabel." I stared into her eyes. "You're in my heart every moment."

She bracketed me with her arms and legs, drawing me closer. "Love me, Drake," she whispered against my mouth. "Love me like you'll never let me go."

"Never again," I promised. I thrust. Slowly at first, and then I pumped faster and faster. Izabel's nails dug into my shoulders as an expression between anguish and ecstasy crossed her face.

And when she gasped, "harder," feral intensity took over, and I fucked her like a caveman. I pounded, hard, wild, and fast. Her nails scored my skin, and I relished the sting as we culminated in blinding pleasure. I spilled into her. Shoving my face into the curve of her neck, I shuddered with the ripples of my climax.

I was crushing her, and yet she held on tight.

I lifted my head. I stared into her eyes.

Our gazes locked, and, in that moment, the angst of our years apart melted away.

It was midnight when I let Izabel up for air. I couldn't stop touching her, afraid it was a dream and she would disappear. She tensed when I kissed down her belly and lingered on the scar across her bikini line.

"I had a C-section," she whispered.

"I know, baby." I grazed my mouth on the mark one last time before crawling up her body. Bracing on my elbows on either side of her head, I pressed a kiss to her forehead.

"I'm not self-conscious about it." She managed a watery smile. "Especially since…" Her words faded and, instead, she let her fingers communicate what she wanted to say. Izabel stroked the healed ridges of tissue on my back—her soft touch, a balm to my invisible wounds.

"Our scars tell our story," I said softly. "The bad, the good. Our heartbreaks and our triumphs. It's up to us to decide our ending." I brushed her hair away from her face. "Don't know about you, baby, but I'm hoping for a pretty damn good one."

Her eyes glistened. "Me too."

She shifted beneath me and winced. "I'm sore."

I hid a grin of satisfaction. "Want me to run you a bath?"

"I'd love it."

I got into the bathtub behind Izabel. We sat huddled together to enjoy the soothing warmth of the water. My wife was quiet, and I thought she'd dozed off. I'd never been this elated in the past three years. There was truth in that *you never know what you've lost until it's gone*. No way was I doing this to our marriage again. I was not re-enlisting with the

SEALs, nor was I continuing with the task force after we fulfilled our mission.

"Do you think we slept together too soon?" she asked drowsily.

My fingers stroking her arms stilled. "Are you regretting that we did?"

She was silent for three heartbeats. "No. I don't think so."

"Maybe we shouldn't overthink it."

"Maybe we should have talked before we slept together."

I smiled against her hair. "We communicate better when we fuck."

She backslapped my shoulder. "Be serious."

"I am, baby. I know there's a lot we need to work through—"

"And there's the elephant in the room...I'm technically no longer married to you."

"That can be corrected with a few keystrokes."

Her hands glided back and forth through the water but she said nothing. I nudged her gently. "Tell me what you're thinking. Don't shut me out."

"It still angers me how easy it is to mess with people's lives."

"Are you referring to the terrorists or the task force?"

"Both," Izabel huffed.

Instinctively, I massaged her shoulders. "I took care of the first and I'm working on the second. Trust me on this."

"I'm scared."

"Hey..." I gently turned her head so I had her eyes. "I have a good feeling we're gonna make it."

I flashed her my roguish smile.

Izabel rolled her eyes knowing what I was up to, but I was relieved how easily we seemed to be falling back into each other.

"I'm meeting with Doc G again in a couple of days," she said.

"So the sessions are helping?"

"I guess."

"Good."

"Do you know when Marcus and I can go back to work?"

"Let's talk about that over dinner."

"It's midnight."

"I'm starving. You?"

"I am too."

HALF AN HOUR LATER, I was in the kitchen in a good mood and whistling as I popped the takeout containers of pasta in the microwave to reheat. Though my stomach was grumbling for food, all I could think about was taking Izabel back to bed. Three years of celibacy finally ended and it was fucking amazing.

Sinking into Izabel's tight heat was every bit the heaven I remembered. My poor wife might not be able to walk tomorrow.

"Iza!" I hollered from the kitchen. "Food's almost ready." My wife and her beauty routine. She mentioned something about putting on a face mask. I guessed having had a mother whose business dealt with beauty ingrained in her certain habits. Not that I was complaining. I remembered how ridiculously unreal her skin felt whenever she did one of her "sandpaper spas" as I teased her about it. Although Izabel insisted it was called exfoliation.

My spine tensed when the sound of a vehicle reached me before its headlights swept over the window. I dropped everything I was doing and opened the cabinet beneath the sink where I hid my Sig.

I headed for the door and peeked behind the curtains. I wasn't alarmed. I had an inkling of who our midnight visitor was. But I was far from complacent or relaxed. The porch lights illuminated two familiar black SUVs.

Viktor stepped down from the driver's side of one vehicle. I could feel his eyes lock on to where I stood. The legend of Viktor Baran transcended all special ops circles. Some say the man wasn't human and maybe a closet superhero. I was inclined to believe it. I'd seen the man in action more than once. But every superhero had his kryptonite, and if Viktor ever had one, it was his wife. She made him human. Which was why I suspected that in his gruff way, Viktor had a stake in me winning Izabel back.

The woman in question chose that moment to make an appearance.

Footsteps scraped on the porch steps, followed by a rap on the door.

"Who is it?" Izabel stayed at the bottom of the staircase, looking apprehensive.

"It's Viktor."

I opened the door. Edmunds, Brick, and Marcus were with him.

"What are you guys doing here?" I asked.

"Marcus!" Izabel gasped as she rushed forward. I blocked my wife before she could get past me and out the door. She was wearing damn sleeping shorts, for Christ's sake.

Brick gave Izabel an appreciative once-over.

"Hey, eyes to me," I growled at my friend, who gave me a lecherous smile.

Motherfucker.

"Overprotective much?" Brick teased.

"Fuck off."

Traces of amusement flashed across everyone's faces.

"Shit's gonna hit the fan tomorrow," Viktor informed me. "Wanna invite us in?"

I glanced over my shoulder at Izabel. "Throw on a robe."

Izabel nodded, her face scarlet. She wasn't wearing a bra either.

My team and Marcus entered the house.

"Man, your wife is a looker…uhm…wow…that…" Brick's gaze followed Izabel's hourglass figure up the staircase.

"Brick, if you say another fucking word…" I started menacingly.

"What? Just saying…know where you're coming from, bro," the ginger-haired operator said. "Why you fought so hard to get back to her."

"Okay, so let's cut the bullshit and tell me why this can't wait 'til tomorrow," I muttered.

"Because tomorrow, the world will know that you survived your team's massacre," Viktor said. "The public will not be privy to classified information, but your return will certainly cause controversy, and I imagine your relationship with Izabel will be under scrutiny."

I crossed my arms. "I get to be Drake Maddox again in public? No more sneaking around?"

Viktor nodded.

My mouth thinned. "Wouldn't that put Tierney and whoever she's working with on alert?"

"That's the idea. We're sure Tierney is involved, but someone's holding the leash."

"She's been in contact with Exetron Oil's CEO, Lawrence Mitchell, through official channels," Brick said. "The news breaks at oh-six hundred. We've locked in on Tierney and Mitchell's signal clouds. Tim is also working on their access to several messaging platforms and will continue to monitor."

Brick's eyes shifted beyond my shoulder and I knew that could only mean that Izabel was back. I cleared my throat and glared at my friend. Brick shrugged and looked at the floor with a secretive smile that I wanted to wipe off his face.

"Marcus," Izabel whispered and this time I didn't stop her from greeting my former commander. After their hug, though, I pulled her back to my side.

"What's going on?" Izabel asked.

I gave her a summary.

"No more hiding?"

"No more hiding," I affirmed, then cut a glance at my team. "I'm concerned with how this will affect Izabel's safety. There were no event triggers when Hamza was killed, correct?"

"That we're aware of," Viktor murmured.

I narrowed my eyes.

"We can't be one hundred percent sure, Maddox, and you

know it. Why we took Izabel the same time we needed to bring Marcus in."

"Okay, then I'll be Izabel's bodyguard," I said.

Marcus cleared his throat. "I believe that's my job."

"Not sure I trust you after Brick and Edmunds got the jump on you."

"Drake," Izabel chided sharply.

"If Mitchell and Tierney are going to make a play, we need to keep everything business as usual," Viktor said.

"Sorry to contradict you, boss...press is gonna have a field day with this story," Edmunds spoke up for the first time. "Nothing's gonna be business as usual."

Viktor shot the Guardian a look of irritation. "Agreed." He turned to me. "But you can't be in your wife's space all the time."

"I am not risking Izabel."

"He can play the devoted husband," Brick suggested. "Totally understandable, right? Some might question why Drake doesn't whisk her away after having been gone for three years."

"Fan-fucking-tastic idea," I muttered.

"She can't abandon the Solace project. It's high profile and at a critical stage," Viktor turned to Izabel. "Am I right?"

"Yes," she responded slowly. "But why do you care?"

Viktor's face was bland, but he was watching Izabel in an assessing way I didn't like.

"No," I growled.

Viktor raised a brow.

"You're not using my wife as bait."

"What's going on?" Izabel grabbed my hand and I instinctively wrapped my arms around her. "Am I missing something?"

"It's nothing, baby. Viktor and the others were just leaving."

The man in question made no move to leave.

"Tierney and Mitchell may not have directed the attack on our operators," Viktor said. "But as far as we know, Tierney breached operational security that wiped out an entire JSOC team. The buck doesn't stop with her. She's the chief of staff of a presidential candidate and I'll be damned before I put any more of our military in this kind of danger."

"Are you sure the Veep isn't involved?"

"VP is a boy scout," Viktor muttered. "He checked out and there's no reason to suspect he's involved."

"You think I can help?" my wife asked.

"Iza." The last thing we needed was to give Viktor an inch. "I don't want this to touch you."

"Just be prepared for them to find your weakness, Maddox."

The man's ice-blue eyes glanced briefly at Izabel, making me bristle. "Your return will raise questions from every corner of the government. If the Navy or JSOC gives you problems, let me know. My people will handle your release from the military. You work for me. We've got Exetron communications and Mitchell and Tierney under close surveillance. We'll handle them. Just do your part."

"Back the fuck up," I growled. "I didn't spend three years separated from my wife, only to turn around and put her in danger. No fucking way."

"Drake—" Izabel started.

"No!" I roared at her with more force than I intended, making her jump. But her eyes flashed, indicating her own rising temper.

"You"—she gritted through her teeth—"unilaterally decided to fake your death in order to keep me safe. I want this to be over. I want every single one of them brought to justice and if I can help in any way, I will. Got it?"

"Mitchell is a cutthroat bastard," I argued.

"You can be too," Izabel said. "Be cutthroat, I mean. Not a bastard."

Brick coughed. "Oh...don't know about that."

Izabel smiled at my teammate, whose face grew as red as his hair.

Jesus. The situation was spiraling out of my control.

"We need to talk about this," I informed my wife, even as it was a struggle not to yell at everyone and kick them out.

Viktor slipped a memory stick from his pocket. "Details are here. We're not sure when, where, or how Tierney and Mitchell will handle this, so we'll play it by ear."

"Oooh..." Izabel looked excited as she stared at the flash drive. "Is this one of those that will self-destruct after you look through it?" she asked, deadpan.

I rolled my eyes as everyone chuckled.

"You guys gotta leave." I scowled at them. "I'd like to spend some time alone with Iza before all this shit goes down."

I ignored my team's knowing looks and herded them to the exit. When the door closed behind the guys, I clasped Izabel's shoulders. "Don't ever, ever give Viktor an opening. For anything."

"I was trying to be helpful."

"Guess what, Iza, you're not," I snapped. "Can't concentrate on my fucking job if I'm worried about your safety."

Izabel shrugged my hands off her shoulders and backed away. "You're such a hypocrite." She pointed between us. "This is what we get when we sleep together and haven't sorted out our problems."

"Not seeing a problem here. Seeing a problem when my wife wants to put herself in the crosshairs of the enemy."

"Well, it's done," she countered.

"I just want to keep you safe," I rasped in growing frustration.

Sadness flashed across her face. "Think about what happened the last time you did that."

I walked right into that one.

"I've made my point." She spun around and headed toward the stairs.

"Aren't you hungry?"

"I've lost my appetite." She continued up the steps.

"Can I sleep in your room?" I called after her.

Izabel flung an arm out and flipped me off.

I grinned. Yeah, I was sleeping with her.

chapter **fifteen**

IZABEL

I awakened slowly and felt eyes on me. My muscles tensed only to relax when I registered Drake's slate-blue eyes. It immediately transported me to happier times. Anxiety surfaced. I was afraid that this was a dream.

"Tell me I'm not dreaming."

"I'm real, baby."

I traced his jaw. "I remember this."

"My creeper tendencies?"

I laughed lightly and switched to my side so we were facing each other. "I wouldn't call you a creeper, but you get this intense look in the morning."

"How intense?"

"Like I'm your world."

"You are, Iza."

We stared at each other for long moments, eyes yearning for each other, but there was still an underlying fear of failing to return to what we once were.

"I'm sorry I brought up what you did again last night," I murmured.

"I understand."

"No. I need to make an effort not to hold on to my anger. I swear, I understand you more now, but the hurt is just hard to escape."

"It's only been a week. I'm prepared to wait it out." He hitched his shoulders. "There's never gonna be anyone else."

I sat up, hugging my knees. "You sure about that?"

"Yup." He narrowed his eyes. "And if you think there's going to be someone else for you, you've got another thing coming."

Because he had me watched.

And just like that, the pain came back. Although muted, it was still the worst day of my life that would be forever etched into my soul.

"I need to get ready for work."

I scrambled off the bed and made it as far as the bathroom door before Drake spun me around and hauled me in. Tears spilled down my cheeks, wetting his chest. A silent cry, one borne from the sad memory, shook my body.

"I'll make it up to you, baby. Just give me this chance."

All I could do was nod. There was fear, but that fear had been overshadowed by a deep resolve to make our marriage work.

It was and always had been Drake.

———

Reporters lined the front of the Stockman and Bose building.

"Oh my God, Viktor wasn't kidding," I mumbled. Marcus had called and given us a status report of what to expect when we got in. Luckily, the underground parking was closely monitored and only employees and clients were allowed through.

Marcus said their security department wasn't happy, but Virginia Beach was a SEAL community and a back-from-the-dead story was sure to make big news.

"...a Navy SEAL who was thought to have died in the Syria JSOC massacre is alive. Details are still emerging, but rumor has it that he's become a real-life James Bond and tracked down and destroyed the terrorist responsible for wiping out his team. We're here in front of his wife's workplace to get a statement on this reunion that can only be made for movies. Izabel Maddox has been in the news lately for her philanthropic work with the Solace Foundation..."

Drake switched off the radio as he drove the SUV into the underground parking. "Tired of hearing the same news over and over."

As for me, I was apprehensive about facing my coworkers. Would they treat me any differently? Drake reached for my hand and gave it a squeeze. "It's gonna be okay."

When the elevator doors opened, Marcus was already waiting for us. He was dressed in a suit instead of his usual cargo pants and tee. He had on an earpiece with the wire disappearing behind his neck.

"Very secret-service like," Drake drawled.

"Fuck off, Maddox."

They greeted each other with a man hug.

"Izabel, you okay?"

"Yes. I thought you were exaggerating when you said there were a couple of news vans out front."

"Izabel!"

We turned to the blonde barreling toward us. Cindy plowed into me and hugged me tight. "We were so worried about you!"

She eyed Drake critically. Then, turning back to me, she mouthed, *He's hot.*

Rolling my eyes, I made the introductions. "Drake, this is Cindy Lake. Cindy, my husband—"

"Drake Maddox," Cindy finished. "Can you be any more caveman by abducting Izabel and Marcus? You gave us quite a scare! Initial reports said it was the Fuego gang and they'd probably beheaded Marcus and sold Izabel to human traffickers."

"Wow," Izabel chuckled. "I didn't know the news was that bad."

Both Marcus and Drake were nodding.

I frowned. "It was that bad?"

"Yes." Cindy linked our arms together and we walked toward my office.

"I want to talk to Marcus about building security…you gonna be okay?" Drake called after me.

"Yes…" I waved him off. "It seems our floor is covered." I pointed to a man sitting near a planter who I recognized as one of Marcus's crew.

Then I was mobbed by my coworkers, and I had to exercise patience as I answered their questions several times over.

Twenty minutes later, I finally made it behind my desk while Cindy returned to hers, so we could actually do some work. A ton of emails needed my attention because Drake had only returned my phone this morning. I made an appointment with Doc G for the next day. Drake and I were making progress, especially after visiting Angelise's grave, but there was still that lingering fear on my part of losing him again.

My door opened, and I expected to see Drake telling me he was leaving.

It was Kyle.

He closed the door behind him as he entered.

"Kyle."

I eyed the closed door nervously. Drake's possessiveness had not changed. And because of the lingering angst over our relationship, it had only become worse. I didn't fear for my safety, but for Kyle's. And I had no desire to have my husband thrown in jail for assault.

Kyle hurried to my side.

Drake was somewhere in the building.

This was a disaster on so many levels.

"God, Izzy. Are you okay?" He hauled me to my feet and dragged me to his chest. His breath fanned my hair. "I was so worried about you."

"Kyle..." I tried to shove away, but Kyle gave me only enough room so he could search my eyes.

"Is he holding you against your will?" he asked.

"Drake? Of course not." Indignation rocked inside me. "That's the most ridiculous thing I've heard."

"Are you saying you and Marcus went willingly with him?"

"Uhm…"

"I had the incident investigated," Kyle stated grimly. "People talk given the right price. The news got it wrong."

Oh shit.

"There was a misunderstanding. Let me go, Kyle," I begged, stealing another anxiety-ridden glance at the door, which Kyle noticed.

"He's with Marcus," he assured me. "Are you afraid of him?"

"No, I'm afraid for you!" I said, frustrated.

Kyle chuckled bitterly. "I can take care of myself."

He held me tighter. "I'm here, Izzy. You know that, right? I'll help you get away from him—"

The door opened, bouncing against the door stopper.

The forbidding shape of Drake darkened the entryway while Cindy peeked worriedly behind him.

"Did you just say that you were going to take *my wife* away from me, you motherfucker?"

The softly spoken words were delivered with enough menace that Kyle finally let me go, but he stubbornly refused to leave my side.

I looked at Cindy. "Get Marcus." I tried to catch Drake's attention, but his eyes were nailed to where Kyle stood beside me. "Drake…"

I tried to step away from Kyle, but he clasped my arm.

Big mistake.

I took a second too long to react because I didn't know how to diffuse the situation without triggering my husband. And apparently, Kyle had no self-preservation either.

"You don't have to do this, Izabel," he said stubbornly.

Big fucking mistake.

"What is wrong with you?" I cried at Kyle, yanking at my arm. My voice was shrill with hysteria. The blast of rage from Drake slammed into me even before I saw him stalking toward us. "He's my husband."

"You got that right, baby," Drake said in a casual tone. "Maybe I won't kill him."

Drake gripped Kyle's wrist in a way that made him release me. I was pushed to the side, and all I saw was a blur of motion, heard a grunt and the sound of smacking flesh before Kyle went flying into my chair. Drake yanked him right up and threw him over the desk.

I stood speechless.

Kyle ended up on the floor, a pile of groaning pain.

Snapped out of my trance, I screamed, "Stop!"

Drake hauled Kyle to his feet, fisted him by the collar, and snarled, "Stay away from her, or I swear to God, if I find you anywhere near her again…I. Will. End. You."

Kyle chuckled derisively. "Go ahead. Beat me up. Show Izzy what a savage you are."

"Drake, enough. Please?" I walked over to him now and laid a pleading hand on his arm. Hard muscles bunched up with tension beneath my palm.

"What the fuck?" Marcus growled, stalking into the room.

Stalking, it seemed, was common as testosterone levels

clotted the air I was breathing, but I dared not leave the room for a single second.

"Let him, go, Maddox. What the fuck?" Marcus repeated, standing beside the fused men like a referee in a match.

Drake finally released Kyle, who tried to maintain his dignity by huffing and straightening his collar.

"Mr. Collins, can I ask you to return to your office?" Marcus asked.

Kyle tried to look around Drake, but the brick wall that was my husband blocked his view. "I'd take Marcus's advice if I were you."

"Are you threatening me?"

"You bet the fuck I am."

"Goddammit, Lieutenant. Stand down."

I touched Drake's torso, and his arms instantly wrapped around me in a show of possession. If the situation wasn't so volatile right now, I'd give my husband a piece of my mind, but it was like placating a wild animal.

Kyle winced at our united front.

I cleared my throat. "Please, Kyle."

Kyle's gaze softened when it landed on me.

My husband tensed.

"Mr. Collins," Marcus repeated in a much harsher tone.

"This isn't over…" Kyle said in parting. I knew what he was doing. It was reckless the way he wanted to prove that Drake was a violent man who would hurt me.

"You son of a bitch…" Drake growled and lunged forward.

Thankfully, Marcus and I held him back, giving Cindy a chance to drag Kyle out the door.

"Dammit, Maddox. Do you know he could press charges?"

"He had his fucking hands all over my wife!"

"Kyle was out of line," I said. "But did you have to beat him up?"

Drake's nostrils flared, his eyes flinty with controlled rage. "Yeah. I did."

Marcus touched his earpiece and listened. "I'll be right there," he spoke into the mic clipped to his suit. "Mr. Bose wants to see me." He glared at Drake. "Try not to cause any more trouble."

When Marcus left, Drake closed the door and locked it. I watched him warily. He was still vibrating with aggression.

"Drake…" I gulped. "You need to chill."

"You're telling me to chill…" The words rolled on his tongue as if he was testing their meaning.

"Well, yeah." I laughed shakily.

"That asshole had his arms around what's mine—" He took a step forward; I took a step back.

"He was concerned."

"Concerned that I would hurt you?"

A step forward.

Another step back.

"Just generally…" my voice faltered.

"Apparently, he thinks he can take you away from me." Drake's arm shot out, caught my wrist, and yanked me against his chest. His eyes glinted with predatory hunger, making me squirm in a mixture of turned-on and annoyance. "Now why would he think that?"

"I don't know."

"What happened on that date?"

Annoyance won. I shoved him away.

He let me go easily.

After I'd put sufficient distance between us, I slapped my hands on my hips and glared. "You have no right to ask me what happened on that date."

A dark brow shot up mockingly. "I don't?"

His derision irked me more. "No. You do not. As far as I'm concerned, I was free and clear to date and kiss anyone I wanted to."

"You kissed him?"

"You know I did."

Drake erased the distance between us. He stood in front of me, toe-to-toe, but I didn't quail, raising my head, chest heaving.

His eyes dropped to my breasts. I was wearing a scoop-neck sweater that revealed a lot of cleavage.

"Stop staring at my boobs!" I snapped.

Drake slowly raised his eyes, and their predatory glint morphed into heated appraisal. An answering heat bloomed between my legs.

Damn this man for arousing me without even trying.

His lids lowered a fraction. "Did he turn you on?"

"Not answering that."

"Did he make you wet, baby?"

"Go fuck—"

His lips crashed down on mine. Shoving up my skirt, he ripped away my panties. Excitement warred with indignation, but my heart raced as Drake swept me up and planted my bare ass on the cool wooden surface.

Dragging my lips from his, I snapped, "Not here!"

"Yes, here," he growled. Shoving my legs apart, he buried his face between my thighs.

"Oh, God!" His tongue jolted every nerve ending in my body, sending my spine arching. I struggled to silence my moan. I stared at the door straight ahead, then at the dark head moving between my legs. The sight was too erotic. I failed to resist and surrendered to the addictive licks of his tongue.

"Drake…stop…we're…" My orgasm swept through me. I convulsed with the pleasure of Drake sucking my clit. My head fell back. My limbs quaked. A loud moan escaped me, but I didn't care anymore. He enslaved me in the sweetest torture. My legs barely stopped trembling when Drake lowered them.

I braced on my elbows, heard a zipper, saw his enormous erection, and then I was hauled off the table like a rag doll.

My legs wrapped around his waist just as my back hit the wall.

He drove into me.

All I could do was cling to him as he rammed into me again and again. The delicious friction delivered by the thick slide of his cock wrenched another orgasm from me. Drake grunted with each thrust. With one final drive, he planted himself deep, shoved his face into the curve of my neck, and released into me.

My pussy throbbed and clamped around his girth.

As our shudders dissipated and our breathing evened out, Drake pressed into me one more time before he withdrew and lowered me to the floor.

"We…we…" I stuttered, trying to wrap my mind around what happened.

"Fucked in your office?" he supplied. There was not one iota of remorse on his face. In its stead was pure male satisfaction.

"I can't believe we did that," I whispered. I stared stupidly at the cum dripping between my legs. Drake walked away and returned with tissues. He knelt in front of me and began cleaning me up.

"Every time you sit behind your desk, you'll think of me with my face smashed against your pussy, eating and licking every bit of you." He reached between my legs and pushed his fingers inside me.

Both of us groaned. Drake's eyes hooded. "Fuck, baby, this is so sexy." He continued sliding his fingers in and out of me.

I half-heartedly tried to pull his fingers away, but what he was doing felt so good. "Drake, you need to stop."

He removed his fingers, righted my skirt, and stood. Towering above me, he glanced around my office like a beast who had marked its territory. "I feel better about leaving you here with that son of a bitch on the same floor."

"Your inner caveman has gone into overdrive," I muttered. Drake had always been crazy possessive, but this was taking it to a whole new level.

He tipped my chin up. "Baby, I'd say this was pretty tame. I saw red when I saw his hands on you. It was either bloodshed or nailing you against the wall. Take your pick."

"Don't be crude."

His lips twisted derisively. "Maybe I've changed. Past

three years stripped me to my most basic needs. The only thing that's keeping me human is you, and I'm not losing you. Got me?"

"Kyle never stood a chance," I admitted.

Drake's eyes softened and a heart-stopping grin broke through his face.

It made me felt giddy.

I loved him still.

"Walk with me." Drake linked our fingers and, together, we headed to the door. "I wanna assure your assistant you're okay."

I glanced at him questioningly.

"You weren't exactly quiet, Iza." He smirked.

My cheeks flamed as he opened the door. Cindy couldn't meet our eyes and her cheeks were red, too.

"Uhm, Marcus wants to see you…after you're done…" my PA told Drake. "…talking to your wife."

"Thanks, Cindy." Drake grinned charmingly before kissing my cheek. By my ear, he murmured, "I'm keeping your panties."

He reminded me of my pantiless state. Damn him. He touched the tip of my nose fondly, winked at me, and turned to head back to the elevators.

"Ohmigod." Cindy fanned herself. "That was hot."

I cupped one side of my burning cheek in embarrassment. "Were we loud?"

"You were." My assistant laughed and waggled her brows. "You look thoroughly fucked."

"Drake can be such a Neanderthal."

"I was Team Kyle, but woman, I'm Team Drake now. Your husband is fine."

A smile tugged at the corners of my mouth. "He is."

"Do I have to call the cleaning department to sanitize your office?"

"Get back to work, Lake."

Cindy's hearty laugh followed me back into the office.

chapter
sixteen

Izabel

"Drake's here."

Cindy's voice came over the intercom just as he strode into my office. It had been over a week since I returned to work. So far, despite the intrusiveness of the press and the Solace project in full throttle, we managed to spend quality time together working on our marriage. We had our joint session with Gina the night before and, today, Drake was taking me out for lunch...just because.

"Ready?"

"Give me one sec." I reviewed the email to the Solace Foundation chairperson and when I determined it looked okay, clicked send.

I pushed back my rolling chair and got up. Tossing my glasses on the table, I smiled at my husband.

"You look a bit frazzled," Drake murmured after giving me a lingering kiss.

"Tired," I quipped. "Someone kept me awake all night."

His hand settled possessively at the small of my back. "Can't get enough of you, baby."

Drake admitted to Doc G that since his return, he had trouble keeping away from me, which explained our frequent lunch dates. One day, he even showed up at my Solace project site and Marcus had to warn him about interfering in our work.

But I felt the same. The hours away from Drake were difficult. If it weren't for my responsibility for this new development, I'd be all for an idyllic getaway, a place where it'd be just the two of us, reconnecting and making up for lost time. It'd be one hell of a long vacation.

Cindy wasn't at her desk when we exited my office.

"The press seems to have thinned out." There was no reporter in sight when we left the building. Drake clasped my hand and we walked side-by-side on the sidewalk. Bittersweet memories stabbed my mind. Of the times I'd seen sweet couples walking down the street like this and thinking I wouldn't ever get to do that with my husband again.

Because it was missing those small and seemingly mundane moments that hurt the most when you lose them. Like waking up to an empty side of the bed. Falling asleep while watching TV and waking up still on the couch when Drake would have always carried me to bed. The pile of laundry cut in half because it was missing his dirty clothes. It took me a year before I was able to put his clothes in a box. It was only because I had a panic attack and my therapist traced it to my unhealthy habit of sniffing Drake's clothes and realizing his scent was fading.

The universe might have played a cruel joke on us, but it gave us a second chance.

"They're always after the next new story." Drake's glib answer yanked me back from my bittersweet memories.

"Admit it, pal. You glared down at another reporter or threatened them with bodily harm."

"Me?" Drake chuckled. "Now, where did you get that idea?"

"I was there, remember? That 'I know six ways to kill you and make it look like an accident' threat to that XNN reporter?"

"He bumped into you on purpose," Drake growled.

I reminded myself to pick my battles with him. Drake would be forever overprotective. It was embedded in his DNA. The interest of the general press was fading, though there were investigative journalists who continued to hound us. It also helped that the whereabouts of Drake for the past three years were deemed classified and that, in itself, discouraged most reporters.

I'd become so attuned to the change in my husband's moods that I could tell when charged air emanated from him, and it didn't take two guesses as to why he tensed up.

Kyle stood motionless by the corner of the building, staring at us with a cold, impassive face. An expression I'd never seen on him before.

It gave me chills.

Two nights later, I had to work late. One of our clients wanted to move the location of their kitchen cabinets and we had to rework the house plans to accommodate the request. Because the client was paying good money to have this done on time and one of my architects on the team was out sick, I took on the changes myself.

I'd been so engrossed in my work, I forgot the time and next I checked my phone, it was eight in the evening. Cindy had left two hours earlier. The same time I shot off a text to Drake informing him of my late night.

Picking up my phone, I typed a message:

> Almost done. You can pick me up soon. 😊

Instantly, bubbles appeared on my screen.

DRAKE
There in 20.

Drake was brief in text and wasn't one for cute emojis, either.

When I entered the drafting room, the printer had finished inking my changes. I rolled up the plans and stuffed them into a circular tube. On my way to the shipping department, I ran into Gordy, who was my personal bodyguard assigned by Marcus.

"I'm going to the shipping department." The section was in the basement and closed at midnight. It would be good to have the plans on their courier's schedule so the contractor and cabinet maker would have their hands on them before noon the next day.

"I'll go with you, ma'am."

It felt weird being followed around a building I'd deemed safe, but it was the only way Drake would agree to leave my side.

"Drake is picking me up." He sent a recent text that he was stuck in traffic. That meant I could drop off the plans, return for my purse, and maybe spend the extra time to do something productive. Sighing, I slipped my phone into the back pocket of my jeans.

The elevator doors dinged and opened. Three men in maintenance coveralls stood there. Their eyes zeroed in on me as if in recognition. My muscles locked and my heart jackknifed to my throat. Gordy tensed and was already reaching behind him.

Everything happened quickly.

The man carrying the large toolkit swung and struck Gordy on the chin before he could unholster his gun.

I screamed.

He reached for me, but I smashed the hard edge of the shipping tube on his face and heard a crunch.

"Run!" Gordy shouted as he recovered and tried to stop the attackers from going after me, but they were too close. Rough arms caught me around the waist, lifting me, but I fought like a wildcat, reaching behind me, grabbing and twisting what I could—ears, hair, skin.

"Dammit! Stun her," a voice roared.

The man I hit with the shipping tube came at me with a stunner, but I wasn't going to make it easy. Drake taught me self-defense skills long ago. I pushed back against the guy holding me, raised both feet and kicked Shipping Tube man, sending him flying.

Suddenly, I was free. Pain exploded on the side of my face, and I saw stars.

"Coop, goddammit, boss said not to hurt her."

"Too late," Coop snarled. I was thrown over someone's shoulder. I wasn't sure which part hurt more, my face or my ribs. Gordy was on the floor, groaning with blood pouring from his side.

He was shot. I didn't even hear gunfire.

In my daze, I clawed at Coop's back, still trying to fight back. Lightning fried me with unbearable pain until my vision dimmed.

chapter
seventeen

Drake

Traffic on Interstate 64 was a clusterfuck. I was going to end up an hour late. She hadn't responded to the last text I'd sent fifteen minutes earlier.

> Iza?

After five more minutes, my irritation at the traffic turned into concern for Izabel. I mounted the phone on the dock and called her.

Her phone went to voicemail.

I called Gordy, but that also went to voicemail.

A tendril of fear licked down my spine. Viktor mentioned in our briefing that five private military contractors had met with Exetron CEO Mitchell three days before. There was nothing unusual about the meeting because Mitchell hired

PMCs all the time, especially for their oil refinery companies in Africa.

Just when I was about to swipe call again, my phone rang. *Harrelson calling.*

Dread burned in my gut like battery acid. "Maddox."

"They got her."

Crushing fear weighed heavy on my lungs, but I couldn't afford to lose my shit now. With dead calm, I replied, "Be there in ten."

The exit was about a quarter of a mile away. I surveyed the sea of red taillights. "Fuck this." I yanked the steering wheel and pulled to the right lane, barely missing a collision with an RV. Angry blasts from car horns slid off my consciousness as I switched to SEAL mode. Despite all my training, my fingers shook when I brought up the BloodTrak app and registered her signal. The bastards were skirting the interstate and taking Izabel heading west.

Glancing ahead, the shoulder was free. I could go after her and go in guns blazing. Or I could take seven minutes to get to Marcus, get the info I needed with what we were up against, and touch base with Viktor to see whether the AGS boss was aware and had already formed a plan.

Without another thought, I wrenched the SUV into the emergency lane on the verge of the interstate and sped past stopped traffic.

At the swerve for the exit, a siren sounded behind me, but I wasn't stopping, even for a cop.

I had one mission: Get Izabel back.

. . .

Two police cruisers screeched behind me as I made a sharp turn on the street leading to Izabel's building. I slammed to a stop beside a sedan, careful not to block any emergency vehicles already parked.

Marcus was accompanying a backboard down the steps.

Ignoring the shouts from the cops at my flank, I sprinted toward Harrelson.

"Looks like you brought the cavalry," Marcus muttered.

I recognized Gordy. "How is he?"

"He's lost a lot of blood," my friend said grimly.

"Did he say anything about Izabel?"

"No."

Someone tapped my shoulder. I spun around and glared at the cop, who was interrupting my conversation with Marcus.

"You're that SEAL," the man gulped. He had a pasty white skin with freckles and looked like he just graduated from the academy.

"Yeah. Sorry about the chase, but I've got shit going down."

"Sir, are you aware it's a felony to—" Freckle Face started, glancing at the other three cops who had given chase to my vehicle, but were also now fidgeting nervously.

"My wife's been kidnapped," I growled.

The cop's eyes widened as he struggled to find the words to say. "You can report it—"

"Oh, for fuck's sake!" I threw up my hands. All four police officers drew their firearms.

"Holster your guns, dammit!" Marcus bellowed. Stepping in front of me, he pulled Freckle Face aside and explained the situation in rapid-fire speech.

Meanwhile, I checked my phone and saw a missed call from Viktor.

"They're on 460 heading to Richmond," Viktor said when I called him. "Guardians are tracking."

"Mitchell's men?"

"Confirmed."

"You have a plan?" I gestured to Marcus that I was leaving and strode past the officers, who gave me a wide berth.

"Not quite. Harrelson with you?"

"Yes."

"Bring him along."

"His man was shot."

"I'm aware. But he'd want in on this."

"Don't think he's ready."

"And you're too close to the situation."

"I'm not standing down," I snarled.

"I've made my point," Viktor clipped and ended the call.

"You're going after her." Marcus approached, stopped, and stared at me across the hood of my SUV.

"Guardians have a twenty on the vehicle." I paused. "Viktor wants you on the op."

Marcus's brows drew together. "But you don't."

"I can't risk Izabel," I admitted.

"My wife and sons," Marcus gritted through his teeth. "I've already let them down. Give me this chance, Lieutenant."

We stared at each other for long seconds…seconds we had no business wasting. "Come on."

Marcus's eyes flared with the fire of the operator he once was. "Let me get a man on Gordy."

Izabel

My whole body was a mass of aches.

I sat in a chair in a poorly lit room, the bulb of an ancient lamp flickering faultily in one corner. Restraints bit into my skin, arms pulled back painfully, that each fraction of movement became agony. The muscles of my neck screamed with tension and tightness.

And yet I refused to give the lanky man before me any satisfaction.

Lawrence Mitchell wore slacks and a dress shirt. He had a head of white hair with a distinct widow's peak. He had the sort of tan that wasn't from long hours under the sun but from a bottle or a tanning bed. Unkempt black brows slashed over his eyes. He reminded me every bit of a James Bond villain. He flashed me an even white smile. I thought all he needed was gold teeth.

"Let's do this again, Mrs. Maddox, and my men will ease your restraints."

"Go fuck yourself."

"Tsk. Tsk. Such language from a beautiful woman like you."

He was sitting in an opposite chair with no table between us. His legs were crossed nonchalantly, with hands linked in front of a knee. "Your husband. Where was he for the past three years? Who was he working for and who financed it?"

"He hasn't told me anything."

"And yet, you were not surprised to see me."

I could have kicked myself for making that mistake. I had Googled Lawrence Mitchell after I'd heard Drake and the guys talk about him. I wanted to know everything about the person responsible for the death of so many brave men. I thinned my lips, refusing to speak.

"What does your husband have on me?" Mitchell repeated the very first question he asked when they'd woken me up. "He must have given you a damn good excuse…why he didn't choose you—"

"Your tactics aren't going to work—"

"He made you a widow for three years and you've been faithful to his memory, haven't you?"

I didn't answer.

"You're a woman who loves deeply," he continued. "But a man like Drake Maddox—do you think he's been faithful?"

I burst out laughing, ignoring the chagrin and waves of anger coming from Mitchell. Admittedly, my amusement was tinged with a bit of hysteria, because I was close to losing my freaking mind. It helped that I'd built up some hate against Mitchell and Tierney ever since I found out about their involvement. Imagining ways I would cut them down with my bottled hatred.

"You don't know a man like Drake. If you did, you wouldn't have abducted me. He *will* come for me and you *will* be sorry."

He snorted derisively. "What a cliché statement."

He stood and looked at the burly shadow in the corner. "You're stronger than I gave you credit for. I admire that in a woman, but not in someone from whom I need information."

The pitying look he gave me sent a wave of terror that threatened to overwhelm my flagging bravado. Coop emerged from the darkness and dragged a desk beside me. He opened a small black case, revealing columns of syringes. "I abhor torture, but I'm all about incentive. I truly believe you don't have anything useful to give me, but I know who does."

"Wait," I whispered, panic choking me. "What are you doing?"

"There are different interrogation methods," Mitchell said casually. "I don't like blood and I'd hate to mar your perfect skin, so we'll stick to the pharmaceutical kind."

Coop held up a big syringe.

"You're not afraid of needles, are you?"

chapter
eighteen

DRAKE

VIKTOR and the Guardians tracked Izabel to Providence Forge. After receiving instructions from the AGS boss, I drove my Escalade, headlights off, onto an unpaved road and parked behind two black SUVs.

"Gear in the back," I told Marcus. We met behind the vehicle's tailgate. I opened a custom-built compartment and handed him a vest and put on my own.

Marcus gave a low whistle. "Whoa, this is pretty badass." He picked up the special edition H&K submachine gun.

"Sorry, bro, that's my baby," I muttered. "Here..." I handed him two handguns and a rifle. If circumstances were different, I would have laughed at Harrelson's disappointed expression, but levity was nowhere to be found in the situation.

After gearing up, we joined Viktor's huddle with the

team. They were looking at a diagram on his tablet, a layout of the property ahead.

"Tim got us the floor plan of the farmhouse," Viktor informed us. "Brick and Edmunds are scoping INFIL points. Drone shows seven heat signatures. Two perimeter guards. Three inside."

"You said seven," Drake said. "Izabel and—?"

"Suspect it's Mitchell."

"Doing his own dirty work?"

Viktor shrugged. "The clusterfuck he's in? I'm not surprised. No self-respecting military contractor would harm the wife of a brother." He pressed on his earpiece. He was receiving a transmission from either Brick or Edmunds.

I studied the farmhouse behind the cover of the tree line that served as our staging area. It was sitting on maybe twenty acres. My phone buzzed once in my pocket. I slipped it out.

It was a message from an unknown number. Attached to it was a video. Terror unlike I'd ever felt before seized my lungs in a vise as the contents of the recording unfolded.

"Jesus fucking Christ," I said hoarsely. "Jesus…Izabel…no…no…no…"

My wife was squirming helplessly away from a big guy holding a syringe. When the man stabbed her in the neck, I wanted to roar. Izabel's scream was the final hammer that shattered my nerves. My vision misted red as I watched her convulse.

Another message followed. "Let's talk."

"Gonna kill those motherfuckers!" I charged forward, totally feral. Two bodies tackled me. I grappled against them, threw one off, and punched another. Someone grunted.

I found myself pinned. Choking.

The red haze cleared, and I saw Viktor's face snarling down at me. His forearm put pressure on my windpipe. "Get a grip, Maddox!"

"They're killing her!" I snarled back.

"Tyrosine Penthanol. Not. Gonna. Kill. Her."

That didn't sound any better in my crazed mind. It was a torture drug. It caused unbearable pain in the form of fire through the veins like flesh-eating acid.

I wanted to howl, to rage, to cry. I attempted to reel it in, to find that calming center, but I was lost in a storm of fury and despair. Mitchell had found the one thing that would break me and send me to my knees.

Boots scraped the gravel beside us.

"I've got this." Marcus Harrelson appeared above us.

Viktor pushed up and away. I remained on the ground.

Breathing in.

Expelling out.

A hand appeared in front of me. I stared at it for one beat, two beats. I grabbed it, letting Marcus haul me up straight into a tight hug.

My former commander murmured in my ear, "Don't let Mitchell win, Lieutenant. This mission isn't over until we get every single motherfucker who murdered our brothers." Marcus drew back, keeping a hand firmly clasped over my nape to give me a supportive once-over shake. "We'll get Izabel back. Got it?"

I gave a tight nod.

"Hooyah, brother."

"Hooyah…Commander."

I was calm.

We took out the two perimeter guards with simultaneous suppressed sniper rounds.

Mitchell's men never saw us coming.

The team converged through two INFIL points on the one-story farmhouse.

Brick and Edmunds busted through the front door and gunned down two of the mercenaries.

Marcus shot through the window and killed the merc who delivered Izabel's pain shot. I wanted that job, but I also wanted to be the first one to get to my wife. I crashed through the second INFIL point—the window of the same room—just as Marcus took his shot. I rolled, gun drawn and had it pointed at that motherfucker Mitchell, noting that Izabel was slouched on the chair…unmoving and soundless.

I coated my nerves in ice as the compulsion to shoot Mitchell on the spot screamed inside me. My finger feathered the trigger as the other man stared at me in stark fear.

"I should kill you…"

"She's alive," Mitchell said in a thin voice. "She just passed out—"

"Shut up, you worthless piece of shit," I snarled.

Viktor turned into the room, leading with the muzzle of an assault rifle. My gun shook as I grappled between bloodlust and the desire to see this fucker burn for his sins for years to come.

"Maddox," Viktor's voice reached me in the vacuum, and only then did I tear my eyes away from Mitchell as the task force chief tipped his chin. "Got this. Go to Izabel."

Viktor barely finished his words when I snapped out of bloodlust and turned to Izabel. I sank to a crouch, slid the KA-BAR from my boot, and cut the flex ties. She fell limply into my arms and I scooped her up.

Without another word, I walked out of the room. Guardians filing in gave me a nod of sympathy.

"Is she all right?" Marcus asked, coming in through the front door and hurrying over to me.

I couldn't speak through the lump in my throat. I didn't know if it was from relief or fear.

All I could do was stare at my Izabel.

Inhale.

Exhale.

"She's gonna be all right," someone said beside me. "Medic!"

Wetness streamed down my cheeks and splashed on her face.

Izabel's brows furrowed and her lids fluttered.

A pulse of hope pushed away the lingering anxiety. We could finally and truly start our life that was cruelly interrupted three years ago.

"Iza," I whispered.

chapter
nineteen

BLOOD OIL

Crude oil prices soar with the arrest of Exetron Oil CEO Lawrence Mitchell. Charges of treason are being considered by the DoJ for his role in the massacre of JSOC operators three years ago that became the greatest loss of life in a single day in special operations history. Details in the breach of operational security remain classified. Mitchell denies all allegations, saying he never signed off on any agreement between Allison Tierney and deceased terrorist leader Youssef Hamza that would allow Exetron Oil freedom to operate in Africa without threats from terrorist organizations.

Tierney has been released from the hospital after an apparent drug overdose. She was immediately arrested by the authorities upon her release. The Vice President's former chief of staff is alleged to be the mastermind behind the Syrian massacre of Navy SEALs and Green Berets. If proven guilty, she will also be charged with treason.

Is the price of our military lives worth the low cost of oil?

chapter
twenty

Six Weeks Later
Izabel

THE FRONT DOOR slammed and jolted me from what I was working on.

"Iza?"

I quickly closed the file I had open on my computer and stood, excited to see my husband after he'd been gone for two days, while also trying to control the sneaky grin that wanted to form on my lips.

"Baby?"

I hurried to meet him, but Drake had already darkened the entrance of my office at the estate home we continued to rent.

The impatience on my husband's face quickly softened into an expression of sheer pleasure at the sight of me.

My heart stuttered. I'd missed him.

Drake swept me into his arms and planted a deep, crushing kiss against my mouth. He quickly pulled away with a wry smile on his face. "I must say, wife, I'm quite disappointed that you weren't rushing to meet me at the door, seeing as I've been gone for two days."

"I was in the middle of something…"

"Was it more important than saying hello to your husband?" he growled. His eyes tracked down my body as if assessing what I was wearing. A kimono robe covered my camisole and sleep shorts, showing a lot of leg.

My mouth twitched. "I take the fifth."

"You're going to pay for that." He spun me around. My laughter caught at the stinging slap on my ass.

"Ow!" I yelped even as a throb started low in my belly, but it was the smolder in his gaze that made my pussy clench.

I tried to hold him off, but he backed me into the room. A mixture of coyness and excitement dared me to tease the simmering mountain of potent male in front of me. "Drake… now, is that a way to say hello…?"

The corner of his mouth hitched up. "I'll teach you how to say hello, wife."

He lunged, and I sidestepped, his fingers catching the robe that ripped from my body. I squealed with laughter. A hard fuck was in my future, and I did the only thing I shouldn't have done.

Ran.

I dashed around him, out of the office and up the staircase, consciously aware that Drake was following me in swift stalking strides.

"Not a good idea to run, baby," he called.

What was I doing?

By the time I reached our bedroom, I was breathless, not from running away from Drake, but from the intense electric ball of anticipation that charged through my body.

Footsteps sounded behind me.

Drake had removed his shirt and I couldn't help marveling at the chiseled muscles rippling beneath his skin as he unbuckled his belt, all the while holding my gaze captive.

He unbuttoned his jeans and lowered his fly.

My lips parted at the sight of the dusting of hair leading to the bulge behind his boxer briefs.

He pounced.

I playfully shoved at his chest, feeling the rumble of need beneath my palms before he robbed my air. His mouth crashed into mine and devoured me in a savage kiss. His hand dove into my shorts, and he growled in approval upon finding me slick as hell.

He lifted me by my ass. I expected to be fucked against the wall, but was surprised when he carried me to the bed and dropped us on it. I lost his mouth for a hot second. Cool air kissed my pelvis as he removed my shorts.

Then he impaled me. A single deep driving thrust that made me gasp.

But he silenced me with another kiss, and I could only sob into his mouth. He circled his hips and ground into me, rubbing my needy, throbbing pussy. Overwhelmed by the ferocity with how he plundered me, I came fast and hard, blinded in the sheer intensity of my orgasm. My inner muscles were still spasming when Drake lifted my leg and pounded into me.

Wrenching his mouth from me, he rasped, "Can't get enough of you. Never enough." He canted his hips to go deeper, eyes blazing with possession. Again and again, he rammed into me until he thrust one final time and emptied himself inside me with a grunt. He collapsed, pinning me under his weight.

After the shudders of his release dissipated, he rolled to my side and pulled me against him. He pressed a quick kiss to my forehead. "Missed you."

"I can tell." I smiled against his skin that bore a sheen of his exertion.

He squeezed my shoulder. "Did you miss me?"

I sighed dramatically. "I guess."

Drake's fingers dug into my ribs. I jerked because I was ticklish there.

"Stop that." I laughed.

He rolled back on top of me, straddling my thighs. "Did you miss me, sweet Izabel?" The devilish glint in his eyes made me laugh harder because just the threat of getting tickled was enough to evoke that reaction.

His eyes hooded. "I love seeing you laugh." He leaned over and brushed a gentle kiss on my lips. "I love you, baby."

We'd experienced so much healing in these past few weeks. Laughing with all my heart was becoming more frequent, especially with this gorgeous and devoted man at my side. "I love you too, Drake."

Drake

"So, how did it go?"

Izabel's question dragged me out from the sands of sleep. I yawned and hugged her tighter. "Good."

"Good?"

"Jesus, Izabel, I'm tired," I grumbled. "Let your man sleep."

"It's barely eight. Have you even eaten?"

She tried to untangle our limbs, but I only locked her tighter. I smiled inwardly when I heard her huff.

"Tell me what was discussed."

I had appeared at the Senate Intelligence Committee hearing with Marcus Harrelson and Viktor Baran. The public outrage that erupted with the arrest of Lawrence Mitchell and Allison Tierney brought the hammer down on our lawmakers to fix what was broken in Washington.

"Viktor gave them a two-hundred-page report of what was broken in the DoD and the CIA. It's a major overhaul, baby. The enemies are learning to adapt, getting more sophisticated, and our government entities are not flexible enough to address the threats."

"Is anything going to be done about the oil lobby?"

I stroked her hair away from her face. "With the global economy playing a key role in overall security, every company or trade association will be scrutinized in their spending." I went on to tell her what I was allowed to say since it had been a closed hearing. "Big changes are coming to Washington."

Izabel sighed. "Well, let's hope it's not all talk."

I hoped so, too. "Enough about me. How's the construction of the Glen Ford neighborhood coming along?"

"The Solace Foundation has finally broken ground on the apartment complex."

"That's good news."

"Also, it was Kyle's last day today," she added quickly.

"It's about damn time." I kept my voice level and tried to control the anger that rose in me every time I remembered the architect's role in Izabel's abduction. Though Izabel saw him as a victim, I viewed him as an idiot.

"He's really sorry about what happened and apologized again before he left," she said.

I didn't say anything. When Marcus discovered how the fake maintenance guys got into the building, I'd lost my mind. Allison Tierney had been watching Izabel and the people around her, picking out who she could target. She'd zeroed in on Kyle. Tierney's MO had always been "sex as a weapon" and she had a bevy of high-paid escorts who she had used to seduce lawmakers she wanted to blackmail. With Kyle, she used them to swipe his keycard, allowing access into the company. The architect hadn't even found out it had been duplicated until Marcus barged into his office and hauled him off for questioning. It was only through Izabel's pleading that kept me from beating the shit out of the guy.

I was also in awe at my wife's resilience from her ordeal. Although the first week or so brought her nightmares, she was able to put the incident behind her with my help and Doc G's.

She was a true-blue SEAL wife.

Izabel's foot rubbed against my legs.

"Cold?" I murmured.

"Hmm…" She pressed closer. "Just miss the feel of you."

"So, what took you so long to get to the door?"

"Not this again," she groaned, giving an emphatic, pained sigh.

"What are you hiding from me?"

She swatted my chest. "What makes you think I'm hiding something?"

"Because you had this smirk on your face and I know you well enough that you're keeping a surprise from me."

"Well, if you know it's a surprise, why are you pushing me about it?" she groused. "What if I'm not ready to show you?"

I barked a laugh. "Well, now, you'll really have to show me."

I tightened my fingers around her rib cage.

"Ugh! You're so annoying." Izabel scrambled away from me, scooted off the bed and snagged her sleep shorts off the floor, and hopped into them. "Well, come on then."

I chuckled as I followed my almost naked wife down the hallway, down the stairs, and into her office.

She snagged her robe off the floor and put herself into it.

"I was enjoying the view," I murmured.

Izabel glared at me before she plopped in front of her computer and woke it up. Her expression grew tender when she clicked on a file and displayed its contents on the screen.

A ball of emotion formed in my throat.

I swallowed hard. "You did this for us?"

"Yes, it was time to draw our new beginning."

epilogue

Two Years Later

Drake

The steaks sizzled on the grill. The patio was hopping with activity. Children were playing in the pool, parents keeping an eye on them...mostly...while the rest of the visitors lazed on lounge chairs, drinking beer or fruity drinks.

"Man, that's some grill you have there." Brick blew a low whistle and handed me a beer.

"Thanks." I welcomed the cool drink by taking a mighty swig.

"I want mine bloody." My friend cheekily put in his steak request before shifting his eyes back to the sixty-inch grill. It was built into a stack of natural stone and was the centerpiece of the outdoor cooking station. To the left of the grill was a stainless-steel top that could serve as a dining area and on the right was a smoker, also built into the structure.

"Must have cost you a pretty penny to put this in."

I smirked. "Helps to have a wife who's well-connected."

"Is Maddox bragging about his grill?" a voice spoke behind us.

I spun around, my grin widening. I dragged the newcomer into a one-arm hug. "Hank, brother, so fucking glad to see you."

"Wouldn't miss the housewarming or the MadDog special," Hank said. "Must say, you've gone all out with the house."

"It was all Izabel." Building our dream home evoked an ever-present excitement and happy ache inside me because it marked the many milestones of our way back to each other. The house had a similar design to the Georgian we'd lived in prior to moving. We'd put a lot of thought into the outdoor space, making sure the sunroom could accommodate Izabel's plants like her orchids. She'd begun collecting them again and the Cymbidium I'd gotten for her became her new favorite. The slate patio had a fire pit that could convert into an area for a hog roast. Which was why a barbecue was the perfect party to celebrate the culmination of our dreams after an unexpected delay.

The delay being the precious bundle that was squirming in Izabel's arms.

Our one-year-old daughter, Ana Lisa Carmen Maddox, named after Izabel's mother and a spitting image of my wife.

When Izabel approached, I quickly turned back to the steaks and flipped them before handing the tongs to Brick.

"Watch them. These should be medium. I'll throw on the next batch later."

"Hey, Hank," Izabel greeted.

"Look at that little one," Hank replied. "Thank God, she looks like you and not Drake."

I pretended to scratch my cheek, but gave him the finger.

Izabel laughed. "Me too."

"Hey." I mock-glared at my wife.

"But if we have a son, I want him to look like his daddy."

Daddy.

Could my heart clench any harder with so much love for my family?

"So where are you off to after this stop?" I asked. "You've gone nomad for a while. Still tired of Garrison?"

Hank chuckled. "Nah, I miss his ugly ass and the team. But I got business to take care of in Sonoma and I'll be swinging by LA first. Then we'll see."

"How much longer until the steaks are ready?" Izabel asked, getting back into hostess duty. "I need to tell Cindy to get the sides out of the oven."

"Another twenty minutes for the next batch." Cooking steaks for a crowd was no easy feat. Everyone had their preference for how they wanted their meat, but I refused to cook well-done steaks except for kids below the age of fifteen.

"Poor Marcus is on lifeguard duty." Izabel looked toward the pool at my business partner. "And looks like he needs a beer."

"Here, let me take her," I offered. Izabel gratefully handed our daughter over and walked away to check on our guests around the pool who were mostly her coworkers from Stockman and Bose.

Harrelson and I started our own security business a few months ago. Task Force Deadly Spear was disbanded after Mitchell and Tierney were charged with treason.

"Where's Viktor?" Hank asked. "Heard a lot about him, but never seen the man."

Brick barked a laugh. "He would never be caught dead at a barbecue."

"Yeah, he likes living in the shadows if he can help it," I murmured.

Everyone chuckled, but there was a truth that the AGS boss man had no patience for family get-togethers unless his wife forced him to attend one and play nice.

I hadn't heard from Viktor since the senate hearing. Though I felt a measure of relief that I got to spend plenty of time with my family...once a SEAL, always a SEAL.

However, after my experience living life as a ghost, I relished this normal life and there was nothing more normal than having a barbecue with family and friends.

LATER THAT EVENING, I tidied up the kitchen, unloading the dishwasher while Izabel put Ana Lisa to sleep. The barbecue was a resounding success and, thankfully, I didn't have to lecture anyone regarding the proper way of cooking a steak because I'd had not one complaint about the MadDog special. Although that could have been because Izabel's coworkers were afraid to criticize her SEAL husband.

It'd also been great to see Hank, and I would have loved for him to stay overnight and catch up, but he had several stops to make in the SEAL community before he headed for the West Coast. I owed a lot to him in keeping me sane these past three years I couldn't be with Izabel.

A sound like a car door closing reached my ear. I carefully lowered the plate I was holding, opened the cabinet directly above me, and pulled out the Sig. I checked the round in the chamber before I lowered it to my side. Moving quietly to the staircase, I listened for sounds of activity. I heard Izabel singing to Ana Lisa.

Protectiveness surged through my system. If that was a thief, he picked the wrong house to rob.

My ears picked up the scrape of boots on the pavers and before I could sneak up on the door, the knock came.

I was familiar with that staccato rap.

Irritation and relief battled inside me. I double-checked our visitor through the peephole and confirmed his identity.

I threw open the door to Viktor Baran.

A ghost of a smile played on his mouth, but I suspected the man was feeling amused because of the irritation on my face.

"Good evening, Maddox."

"Jesus, Viktor, ever heard of texting?" I waved my arm to let him in. "I could have shot you."

"You're not that reactive."

I pointed to the second floor. "My world is up there. I don't give a shit if I'm overreacting as long as they're safe."

"Nice house," Viktor remarked as though I hadn't just given him the third degree about showing up unannounced.

But this was exactly how this man operated—in the shadows—and I knew if Viktor really wanted to sneak up on us, I wouldn't have heard a sound.

"You missed a good barbecue," I told him.

"Not fond of them."

"Why are you here?"

"No!" Izabel cried. She flew down the stairs and ran right up to us. Before I could stop her, she inserted her tiny frame between Viktor and me. "You're not getting your hands on him again."

"Izabel." My fingers grabbed her shoulders and pulled her against me. "I've got this."

She spun around, color heightened, eyes blazing as if she was spoiling for a fight. "I know you do, but I'm here by your side. And I will fight for you."

"That's well and good, baby, but you get I'm the man in this house."

"What does that have to do with anything?" she shrieked.

"It doesn't sit well on my balls that my wife is facing up to a man triple her size trying to protect me."

Her eyes flashed. "Then what's the use of training me in self-defense to protect against men your size?"

I clamped my mouth shut.

Viktor emitted a rare chuckle. "She has a point, and I'd volunteer to test your skills."

"Don't put ideas in her head," I muttered.

"Don't worry, Mrs. Maddox. I just came by to congratulate you on a beautiful house. And I believe I haven't congratulated you both on the birth of your daughter."

Izabel wasn't convinced and looked at Viktor doubtfully. "This isn't a trick, is it?"

"It's not. In fact, Maddox, could you please retrieve the box in my vehicle? Marissa wanted to send you guys something for the house and the baby."

"Why didn't you bring it in yourself?" I asked, baffled.

Viktor grimaced, didn't say another word, and pivoted to walk out the door. We followed him to his SUV, and I realized why Viktor didn't want to be caught dead holding the box.

"My wife's been messing with me," he muttered. "It was enough I had to carry that thing from the loft to the car."

In the cargo area sat a big box wrapped in pink wrapping paper with a unicorn print. If that wasn't enough, a large white bow finished the look. I couldn't help cracking up with the vision of Viktor carrying that thing.

I leaned in and lifted the box from the SUV. "You should try having kids, Viktor. Then you'll get over this aversion to pink wrapping paper."

Fuck off Viktor mouthed as he slammed the back closed and opened the driver's door.

"Care for a drink? Scotch? Beer?"

Viktor shook his head. "Marissa's expecting me back tonight."

"I'm touched," I teased. "You mean you came all the way down from DC just to deliver this?"

Viktor emitted a wry chuckle. "Yeah. Guess I'm getting soft in my later years."

I barked a laugh as the other man started the engine and backed out of our driveway.

"That was a weird visit," Izabel said, bemused as we went inside.

I didn't answer. It was Viktor's personality. Beyond the cold façade that he projected, there was a man who cared deeply.

IZABEL

I SNUGGLED CLOSE TO DRAKE, our bodies still glistening with a sheen of sweat from making love. He loved me slow and sweet, which wasn't our usual style, but, given how hectic the day had been, I welcomed the pace. Usually I'd fall asleep after sex, especially since Ana Lisa sucked up so much of my energy, but the appearance of Viktor had started the gears in my head, trying to understand this sudden peace that had settled in my heart.

"Full circle," I whispered.

"What was that, baby?" Drake murmured drowsily as he shifted beside me.

"There was always that niggle of fear," I said. "I told you this, but this last year, it hasn't been about my trust in you. You've had it. Ever since I drew those plans for this house, I was ready for a new beginning with you."

Drake was silent, then with a heavy exhale, he said, "Not quite following, Iza."

"I didn't trust the people who'd influenced your decision to leave me."

"Viktor?"

"Yes," I confirmed. "I know you've always been annoyed at him, but I see a grudging respect."

"Grudging is right," Drake muttered.

I laughed softly. "He's not all that bad, it seems."

"Is it because he got Ana Lisa that electric car?"

"No. It's because I see how he loves his wife."

"Because he carried that pink box for her? If that's all it takes to prove how much I love you and Ana Lisa, I'd carry a damn pink box every day."

I pressed my body closer. "Have I told you how much I love our life?"

"I'd rather you say you love me." There was amusement in his voice.

I pinched his ab muscle.

"Damn, woman, what was that for?" he mumbled. "Can't help it if your husband wants to hear it all the time…I'm a needy son of a bitch. Deal with it."

"Oh, Drake…"

He moved and covered my body. Propping up on his elbows, he cupped my face as if there was something very important to tell me. "I'm madly in love with you, Izabel. I thought I was crazy for you before, but now you've given me a daughter to love as well. Both of you are my entire life. Nothing is going to take me away from my family. This is forever, baby. You, me, Ana Lisa, and all the tiny replicas you plan on giving me."

"You want all daughters?"

"Son. Daughter. Doesn't matter as long as they're from you, I'll love them."

"Love you, Drake." I touched his chest. "You have my heart…forever."

I hope you enjoyed Drake and Izabel's story.
Curious about the mysterious Viktor? Find out more about his softer side in his book Smoke and Shadows.

Hank's book is Forced Protector. It can be read as a standalone but is part of my Rogue Protectors series.

connect with the author

Find me at:

Facebook: Victoria Paige Books
Website: victoriapaigebooks.com
Email: victoriapaigebooks@gmail.com
FB Reader Group: Very Important Paige readers

facebook.com/victoriapaigebooks
tiktok.com/@vpaigebooks
instagram.com/victoriapaigebooks

also by victoria paige

Scorned Fate

Scorned Heir

Scorned Vows

Scorned Love

Scorned Obsession

Scorned Beauty (Fall 2025)

Rogue Protectors

The Ex Assignment

Protector of Convenience

The Boss Assignment

Her Covert Protector

The Wife Assignment

Forced Protector

Guardians

Fire and Ice

Beneath the Fire (novella)

Silver Fire

Smoke and Shadows

Always

It's Always Been You

Always Been Mine

A Love For Always

Misty Grove

Fighting Chance

Saving Grace

Unexpected Vows

Standalone

De Lucci's Obsession

Deadly Obsession

Captive Lies

The Princess and the Mercenary

Reclaiming Izabel

* All series books can be read as standalone